TANGLES

TWISTS

AND

TURNS

First Published in Great Britain 2022 by Mirador Publishing

First edition: 2022

ISBN: 978-1-914965-69-2

Mirador Publishing
10 Greenbrook Terrace
Taunton
Somerset
UK
TA1 1UT

Tangles Twists and Turns

An "Oodunit" Novel by

Mike Haley

In a small town like Sanderford everybody knew everyone else and all their business. There weren't many crimes committed, let alone murders, so when nasty bully, Henry Burrows met his fate there were suspects galore. Solving the case was a tortuous journey, especially as the two detectives assigned to case were calm, long-serving, play-it-by-the-book, Stuart McPherson, and aggressive, get- a-confession-from-a-dead-man, Alan (Fearsome) Pearson.

?

??

???

????

?????

??????

Chapter 1
Thursday 8th November, Midday
The Beast

"Yes!"

Burrows growled like a Bengal tiger on amphetamines. Then he spotted the outstandingly beautiful Tania at his office door, her hair like black treacle framing her oval face. Every man in the place fancied Tania, except Henry Burrows that is. He was totally oblivious to her charms. It was truly a case of Beauty and the Beast.

The lovely Tania was tall and elegant and perfectly made up and manicured, with a healthy olive skin, green eyes, pearly white teeth and full luscious "Kiss me like there's no tomorrow" lips. She dressed and carried herself like a supermodel, with those dangerous curves and flashing eyelashes. She knew it well and flirted outrageously at every eligible male. She winked at David, smiled and pursed her lips.

"David's here to see you Mr. Burrows." she said.

"Send him in then, girl, don't just stand there gawping."

David entered quietly and shut the door behind him. Burrows was facing the window and studying the pigeons on the opposite roof.

"Rats with wings: that's what they are; dirty flying nuisances. I'd poison the bloody lot of them."

Burrows carried on being ignorant while David stood and waited in the heavy silence. He'd worked at Bridges Construction and Planning for over five years, and he was completely aware what his boss's behaviour was all about. He knew that he was one of those punchy "Get it done today, and get it done quick, or else." types. His unerring motto, indeed his raison d'être was, "My way, or No way." The Beast had never believed in being nice to people on the way up, because sure as hell, he didn't ever expect to meet anyone again on the way down. Slouching in his black leather upholstered office chair, he turned towards David who was standing a healthy distance away on the edge of a blue Persian rug. He smirked. David grinned and was the very soul of politeness.

"You asked to see me, Mr. Burrows."

It wasn't the first time that David noticed how those eyes didn't look at you. They looked through you as if you were not there. You were just wallpaper. His boss's haughty nose and mouth carried an expression like he was trudging reluctantly through the stench of a pig sty. With every breath, every posture, every word, he let you know, "I don't want to be here, with you."

It was an unusual day for early November, a clammy day, thunderstorms threatening, air heavy and damp like a Turkish bath, not made any more bearable by the fact that in the office of the Beast the central heating was invariably turned up to max. David winced as two beads of sweat dripped off Burrows forehead on to his huge mahogany leather faced desk. He held his breath when he realised that his boss had his shoes off under there. Just visible were his white socks, discoloured in patches of yellow. The office always smelt like Cheddar Caves with a dodgy thermostat.

The Beast of Bridges Construction looked up. Cigarette smoke was leaving in a rapid stream from his nostrils as if he were an angry fire breathing dragon.

"Yes, David," he sneered, his gruff voice like a Johnny Rotten lyric, "I'll come straight to the point."

Then he paused and took a glance out of the window again. There was some undercurrent of delight about his demeanor.

"You are surplus to requirements. Clear your desk and piss off. We don't need you anymore."

Then he turned around back towards the window, and with one foot on the window sill, removed his sock and began to clip his big toenail. David was filled with disgust at his treatment, but he maintained his dignity.

"Thank you, Sir, that's very good of you." he smiled, "I'll be as quick as I can."

Burrows ignored him and David left the office quietly, grinning like a baboon in a banana ripening warehouse. He was glad that the confrontation was over, but it had all been totally unnecessary. It had been not quite the moment of truth he had anticipated, but Mr. Obnoxious Prat had sadly been lost in his own truth of the moment. The victim of redundancy had been planning to resign anyway.

"Silly old sod! He doesn't watch the late evening local news on the telly; otherwise he would have seen me collecting my lottery winner's cheque. There are probably a lot of other people in Sanderford who wouldn't have heard the news yet. That can only be good, but it won't be long 'til they do hear."

Tania gave David a sad eyes expression and asked, "You as well?"

"If you mean have I got the chop, then yes. The Beast has just sacked me."

"Second one today. Mr. Wilson got his marching orders earlier this morning, and he's been with Bridges for over 15 years. He went mental; threatened to twist Burrows' bollocks off."

David grinned, and answered, "Oh, well, every cloud and all that."

Tania continued, "I don't know what's going on, but it looks bad. All the others, the construction workers, were laid off this morning. Some of them have families to support, kids to feed, and now the only thing they can look forward to is being on the dole. But you don't seem too bothered."

"No, I've got something up my sleeve."

"Really, is it a bomb or a shotgun?" she joked, "That ignorant pig would surely deserve to be bumped off. I hate him, I detest him. He's awful to work for, and I'd leave tomorrow if I could, but it's a tough world out there for personal assistants, and I've got the mortgage on my flat to pay."

She paused, gave another of her little girl lost looks, and added, "Do you have a plan then?"

The Lottery winner tapped his index finger alongside his nose, and smiled, "That would be telling."

Anyhow, now he knew that Tania didn't realise yet that he'd had a big lottery win. He left with a wave, saying, "I'm off to the Feathers for my lunch; see you in there sometime."

Chapter 2
Thursday 8th November, Afternoon
The Feathers

Just along Taplow Street, David saw John Wilson going into the Feathers. He followed him in and stood alongside him at the bar.

"So, we are both redundant then?"

He felt that he needed to show a bit of empathy to a long time work colleague, and ordered two pints of Old Rustic Nectar Premium.

They sat down next to the roaring log fire. Judging by the unusual weather it was totally unnecessary to have lit it, especially as John was already well heated up. His face was red and full of anger, but this was not the John that everybody in Sanderford knew, a conscientious, gentle, quiet man.

"I'll get even with that bastard, if it's the last thing I do. I tell you, he's got a nasty surprise coming to him."

"Don't be too hasty John. I'm sure if you wait a while, there'll be somebody else who hates him enough to do the job for you."

"Maybe, but then I wouldn't have the pleasure of seeing him squirm and plead for his life while I rip his bollocks off and stuff them up his arse."

John's voice didn't have any volume control and he was getting awkward looks from the other punters around the bar.

"It's getting a bit too warm in here; let's adjourn to the beer garden." suggested David, "And have a serious talk about this."

They moved to a table by the River Sander and sipped at their beers.

"I've heard a rumour that Terry Lennox is in a bit of financial trouble and is having to close down some of his operations. So that is probably the reason why we are both out of a job." David confided quietly.

"Quite honestly, I don't give a shit." John's voice still raised.

"Is it right that we have to go on the dole, and Burrows stays in his job? You know that when he arrived from Cousins Construction, it was either me or Frank Archer that was earmarked for the post as general manager, but we were both overlooked because Burrows was such a nasty bastard? I don't know what he told Frank, but Terry Lennox told me that I should have got the job, but I was too friendly and nice with the construction workers. Nice! Good word! Exactly the opposite of that contemptuous little shite."

The red faced redundant took a very large swig from his beer, and his tirade ceased for a few seconds.

"So, what will you do now then, John?"

"Oh, I don't know. The wolf is certainly not at the door and Mary's got a good job at Flack, Allen and Crosby. I can afford to take a break and get a part time post if necessary. But we were planning to provide some finance for my grandson Robert when he starts his mathematics degree at the University next year."

"Where's he going to do that?"

"Over at Didmanchester."

"That's good news."

"Yes, but I'll have to rejig the sums now so we can afford it. You probably guess that at my age the mortgage is paid up and we have a lovely house in Burnside Avenue, but this is a real kick in the teeth for me. I could have realised a bloody good pension if I'd done another two years. I don't even know what the redundancy package will be. If Lennox is going bust, it could be peanuts."

"Are you going to look for another job?"

"Yes, but at my age and on my salary it will be difficult. Nobody wants to pay top whack for an architect or quantity surveyor at 54 years young."

There was a pause while the dregs of the ale were keenly supped, then John asked, "What will you do? You don't look all that worried."

"I don't know either, but I've got my age on my side, and I'll survive."

As the lunchtime rush in this favourite Sanderford watering hole built up, it gave the former work colleagues an opportunity to quaff another pint. John wolfed down a chicken and avocado sourdough sandwich while they chatted on, mostly about working for Bridges and what a contemptuous piece of detritus Henry Burrows was. It soon became obvious from the lack of questioning that John also had no idea yet about his friend's lottery win. The sun was shining, the Feathers was booming, and the riverside pub's relaxed atmosphere soon appeared to calm things down.

"Anyway, John, please, don't do anything silly." smiled David, as he finished his pint and made to leave. His companion was clearly not content with two pints and was staying for the duration.

"I'll have a couple more for Dutch courage before I go home and tell Mary what has happened."

"See you at the writer's group next week, then. Regards to Mary and the family."

Chapter 3
Thursday 8th November, Afternoon
Jeffery

Leaving the pub, David went home contented after his couple of pints. His mongrel super mutt was very pleased to see him even if it wasn't at the usual time of day. Jeffery, the faithful hound howled with pleasure; his wonky ears cocked and his feathery tail furiously wagging in anticipation. He looked up with those sad brown eyes, expecting to be fed. He knew that his master would never let him down. Food was ready quickly. Jeffery offered a paw as David patted him warmly and said, "Good Boy". That was the signal. The grateful mutt took two steps towards his feeding bowl and greedily devoured the contents in no time at all. Jeffery was happy again. He jumped up, settled back on the sofa contented and closed his eyes.

"My life is easy. I am pampered, brushed and well fed. I only have to show my human master how clever I am by repeating the same old tricks I learned years ago, and I know I will be rewarded with a biscuit or a meaty treat. If I wag my tail and give one of those pleading looks, I can get anything I want; food, walkies, stroking; anything. When he is here, this is my happy home. I like living here.

But around about every seven of my canine years something happens to these humans that I don't understand. They call it a celebration, but it just makes me shake and cower in my basket. So many loud bangs and whistles; one after another. Sometimes it goes on for weeks. I do a lot of barking and try to show that I am brave, but really I am frightened, my ears hurt and I wish it would stop. It happened again only a few days ago, and I'm only just getting over it now.

Apart from that I don't have many problems. I have my favourite spots in the sun when it's warm and by the fire when it's cold. One thing that does get my goat though, and I don't really know why, is when the letter box clatters and paper things come through the door. I think maybe it's because they're trying to invade my territory. If I get there first, then I'll make a big fuss, barking and growling. I hate newspapers and try to rip them to shreds. Luckily the master jokes about me having read the paper first. The lady of the house isn't so understanding, especially when I rip letters up. She puts her slippered foot right up my bum and shouts, "Go away!" My man does his best to quickly calm her down, and it is soon all quiet again.

Nothing much surprises me, I've seen it all now, but occasionally they spring one on me. It happens when I've got my coat all nice, dirty, and matted, probably because I've been in the river or rolled in something lovely and smelly. I'm happy and contented. They pick me up and throw me in a bath of hot water and bubbles that make me smell like them. This is not a nice surprise for me; I hate it, but I always reward them by shaking myself from head to tail and drenching them in the process. Who is surprised then?"

Chapter 4
Thursday 8th November, Afternoon
Walkies

It was walkies time, and David decided to take Jeffery for a long walk through the park and then along the River Sander, and to work out what he was going to say to Brenda when she got home from her job at the local Poundshop.

It was an odd situation, because in normal circumstances he would have had both good news and bad news. So far it appeared that Brenda had no idea that he had won the lottery. Perhaps that was the good news? If they had not endured a very stormy relationship for the last three years, then it would be very good news and she would be delighted. But they had often had rows, fights, trial separations and had gone to Relate twice, which only resulted in very temporary fixes. Throwing in the towel had been brewing for a while and now, there was a way out of the relationship. The bad news, of course, was that he had lost his job at Bridges, and again, if they were really a "together" couple, she would be very worried about that.

While David was mulling it over all along the riverbank, Jeffery was busy sniffing away and cocking his little leg in all the best places.

"If she doesn't know about the lottery win, then she will know soon. That's the way things go in this town." he thought to himself.

"I'll tell her tonight that she's on the skids and I'd be suing for divorce if we were married. Good thing it's only a civil partnership with no contract between us and so that will be easier. It's my flat, so I'll do a Burrows on her."

He smiled at the thought and then considered, *"If and when she finds out about my new good fortune, I'll tell her that I owe her nothing."*

As they strolled along, the crisp evening air began to hide among an accumulation of billowing rain clouds behind the Bellowmead Hills and there was a sudden chill in the air. The contrast with the almost summer warmth of the morning was striking. Jeffery would have walked on contented for another few miles, but when man and dog got to the Hollingwood lock, the skies had darkened to threaten a rain storm. They turned back just as the swish of wind in bare willow trees seemed to signal the need for a rapid change of plan. Sure enough, only a few yards disappeared under their footsteps before the wind swirled in an angry maelstrom and rain began to fall in a freezing winter shower. Within a minute, the rain gave way to hail, and they were forced to backtrack and take shelter under the porch way of the derelict lock- keeper's house. It was miserable and cold.

"Bloody British weather!" David moaned out loud. After a 5 minute wait, he decided there was no other option but to brave the storm and hurry back home. He wasn't altogether sure, but through the rain obscuring the view in his spectacles, he thought he saw John Wilson asleep on a bench by the bushes near the duck pond. He was in no mood to confirm his sighting by going over and waking him up because he was already drenched. The dog and walker arrived back looking like a ragamuffin and his faithful but drenched mutt, Jeffery, dried himself with a shake and a snooze as close to the radiator as he dared, while David stripped off his saturated clothes and took a shower. He had returned downstairs to the kitchen and put the kettle on for a nice cup of hot chocolate when he heard the door slam.

"You bastard!" Brenda cried out, "You bastard! Why didn't you tell me? It's all over this fuckin' town that you've won two million on the lottery last night. Why am I the last to know? And you didn't feel the need to let me know that Burrows had done the dirty on you this morning. I suppose you think that just because you're redundant now, I won't get half of your winnings. We've been together for over five years and you fail to communicate important stuff to me. I'm as good as a wife to you, and you treat me like a piece of shit scraped off your oversize shoes."

David just sat there and smiled, waiting for his moment after the machine gun tirade had subsided. The angry partner stood fuming and waving an accusatory finger at him as she built up to a fine lather, almost to foaming at the mouth with rage. He let his mind wander as she went on and on and on, and then she stamped her foot and stormed off into the kitchen.

He remembered the previous weekend, when he was sure she had wanted to humiliate him. He even wondered if she had perhaps attempted to kill him.

Brenda had two passions in her life and one of them was certainly not David. She was obsessed with interests that were at least tenuously connected. One was geology and the other was rock climbing. David showed a polite interest in the geology, but was more interested in heavy rock like Guns and Roses and Black Sabbath. As far as rock climbing went, he had an overwhelming fear of heights. So the last straw for him as far as the long term "love affair" with Brenda went, was when she insisted on taking him to Carlison's Rocks, a nearby sandstone outcrop. She had agitated and cajoled him into attempting a climb.

"i always knew you were a whimpering coward," she taunted, "Pull yourself together and act like a hero."

He remembered how he had eventually acquiesced and how terrifying the experience had been. Brenda had climbed swiftly to the top of the crag and left him dangling on a rope half way up. He had scrambled shaky and breathless to the top, only to find that she had disappeared.

He thought, perhaps a little too pleasurably *"Perhaps she had fallen."*

There was no way out of the dilemma, other than to go back down. It seemed to take ages for his knees to stop shaking and his fear of heights to subside, while he endured the slow descent down the rock face over every terrifying nook and cranny. When he reached the safety of level ground at the bottom of the crag, he was puzzled. There was no sign of her. He searched every crevice and behind every boulder, and then he looked up and heard her voice taunting him again, saying, "I'm up here, you dimwit. Why aren't you brave, like a real man?"

The warring couple never spoke a word to each other all the way home in the car, and then after a short row, Brenda slammed the door at the flat and without a word sloped off to see her friend Sharon. When he woke up the next morning, David realised she had stayed the night over at Sharon's flat.

That had been it, the watershed, the final insult, and David's mind was then made up to extricate himself from the partnership at the earliest opportunity. Now Brenda's new outburst had made him even more sure of the path he wished to take.

After a few minutes, Brenda came back into the lounge while David was watching football on the TV. "Turn that shit off, you moron. I've got something important to say."

Chapter 5
Thursday 8th November, Evening
A bombshell

David carried on watching the TV, ignoring her, and so she flew across the room and pulled the plug. Then she sat back down and poured herself a tumbler full of cheap red wine, took a huge swig and uttered:

"OK. Now I've got your attention, it's time for some truth."

"So what have you got to say then?" he asked, "Only, can you get it over quickly, 'cause Liverpool are two nil up in the semi-final and I want to watch the rest of the match."

She sighed indignantly and took another swig followed by a deep breath.

"Me and Sharon have been talking, and I've made a decision."

He hoped she would say that it was over and she was leaving him to go and live with Sharon. He just smiled and waited for her to spout again.

"I've made a very important decision. I don't want to be Brenda anymore. From now on, I want to be known as Brian and I expect you to support me through my transgender process with your ill-gotten gains."

David was disgusted. Brenda, (or was it Brian?) added, "Love me as I am, and as who I want to be or I'll leave you. What am I saying? We were burned in the bushes long ago, so never mind about love, just give me half your winnings and I'll be out of your hair forever."

David made her wait a few seconds before he replied, "There's the door."

She got up, walked across the room and for the second time in a few hours, slammed the door, and then she shouted, "Nothing you can do will hurt me now, but I will definitely hurt you if you do nothing to help."

At half time David reflected on his situation.

"This is a dreadful situation. Because I won't help her become Brian, she's threatened to start "divorce proceedings" on irreconcilable differences and screw me for every penny. Even though we aren't married, she's assumed that as a common law wife, she has the same rights. She seems determined to make it as messy as possible. She wants half of everything and even threatened to have Jeffery put to sleep the next morning. If she runs true to form, she'll want to start a fight. It will be more of a scuffle than a fight, mostly with me trying to protect myself while she rains blows down on me. I expect that after she finally leaves, she will go straight to the police and lie through her teeth to have me arrested again on a trumped up assault charge. She has always been quite capable of doing some stupid and dangerous things. I remember the day when, after a previous round of arguments, she had turned up with her mate Sharon, poured petrol over my car and set fire to it. I don't want to do anything to save the situation. It appears that now the girl of my dreams has turned out to be the witch of my nightmares."

While David pondered the circumstances, worse was to come through the next few minutes, as Brenda returned again and again with "And another thing!" Eventually, at about 7 o'clock she gave up and slammed the door for the last time, shouting," I'm going over to Sharon's."

David was relieved that there had not been a fight. He had kept the TV switched on throughout the series of returns, tirades and threats and was delighted when Liverpool won 4-1.

Later that evening, he had a call on his mobile from Terry Lennox.

"Hi Davy boy! I'm sorry about you getting the push."

"That's all very well, but what about John and Tania? Are the rumours about your financial situation true? You know what it's like in Sanderford; everybody knows you, and the bush telegraph ensures they all know what goes on."

Terry let out an indignant sigh and then paused as if he was thinking of something believable to reassure.

"It's bollocks! I'm OK and everything is just fine," he spat, "And it's just about consolidating my portfolio of companies. Come and see me at the house tomorrow morning and we'll have a chat about it. I've got a proposition for you."

"OK, see you about 8.30 then?"

"Perfect!"

Chapter 6
Thursday 8th November, Late afternoon
Footsteps in the park

A long and miserable session in the Feathers had ended abruptly when George, the landlord, decided that he'd better send John home.

"Listen mate, I think you'd better go home. You've been here all afternoon. It'll be dark soon and Mary will expect you back for your dinner. How many pints is it now? Six or seven, I guess."

John groaned and reluctantly downed the dregs of his last pint.

"I suppose you're right George." he slurred.

Walking wasn't easy in his condition, but John decided to stroll home through the Willow Tree Park. It had been many years since he'd managed to swill down so much bitter. He was grateful when he reached what the winter was leaving behind as the remains of the foliage in the park because by that time he was busting for a pee. Dashing behind a bush, he soon let out a contented, "Aaaah!"

The joy was temporary. He was still seething with anger; arguing with himself as he staggered along. He began to think how Mary would react to him arriving home three sheets to the wind and eventually decided to sit down on a handy park bench and compose himself with a few minutes of deep breathing. The bench wasn't comfortable, but he soon dozed off.

"I'd thought about it and worked out all the detail and I knew exactly where I was going to do it. It was plain that bloody Henry Burrows had hated me when I was a contender for his job and now the feeling was mutual. So I have decided that tonight

will be the night that I would sort him out once and for all. I'd taken my best breadknife from the kitchen, sharpened it, and tucked it inside my overcoat.

Here in the Willow Tree Park I crouched, waiting in the bushes down by the lake. Yes, I was going equipped, equipped to kill the snotty, obnoxious little bastard who had so ingloriously sacked me that morning.

A full moon shone overhead and I thought about witches and vampires. Would it be too light to do it? Would someone see me?

I'd removed my work shoes and put on the pair of plimsoles I always carried in my rucksack, so that when I run up behind my prey, he won't hear me coming. I relished the thought of slashing his throat and watching him croak before my eyes. An owl hooted in the bare branches of a willow tree and a group of ducks was happily splashing across the lake.

There he was, looming up towards me in the darkness, brown overcoat, thinning hair, dirty shoes, walking along with that over confident air. He passed me by, as I stopped breathing for a few seconds. I could hear my heart thumping against my ribs. He was ten yards past me as I came out from the bushes and ran towards him. Got him! Slash! Slash! Slash!

He hit the tarmac with a heavy, almost thunderous crash, and began to writhe as blood squirted from his neck. He was choking on his own blood, and I felt relieved and elated. I turned him over to face me, so that I was the last image he had in his eyes before he went to Hell.

He let out a tortured groan and his empty eyes stared at me. I shivered and shook.

"Oh Shit!" I cried, "What have I done? It's not Henry Burrows."

Chapter 7
Friday 9th November, Morning
Lennox makes an offer

Approaching the mansion that was Sandersdale House was an experience David had never enjoyed before. Living in a small flat across town in Newcastle Gardens, he had always envied the way the other half lived. Terry Lennox's place was something else. Wrought iron gates, electronically controlled, opened slowly to let David in and he strode up a long gravel driveway, through delightfully manicured lawns framed by well-tended bushes. The mansion itself was like something out of a Hollywood epic, a James Bond movie pile, pure white with a massive pink granite step to an oak panelled front door. There were three cars on the drive; a blue Tesla, an immaculate black Range Rover and Terry's grey-green chauffeur driven Rolls Royce.

David's lifestyle was much more modest. He kept the flat tidy and clean, furnished mostly from Ikea and he kept himself tidy and clean, wearing good clothes and indulging in good grooming. He had his blonde locks shorn once a month, was clean shaven and freshly deodorised every day. For work he always wore a blue suit, white shirt, black tie and highly polished black shoes. Outside work he was casual, wearing black trainers, Levi jeans and Hollister tee-shirts. However much he looked after himself, he knew he was unable to compete with Terry Lennox.

David thought, *"This guy is most certainly the Lord of the Manor."*

Everybody in Sanderford knew that Terry Lennox was a rogue, a likeable and extraordinarily rich rogue, a council house boy who had pulled himself up by his bootstraps to become the local millionaire businessman. He was the Sanderford poor kid made good. He oversaw a veritable empire; a portfolio of six companies in Planning, Construction, Building Supplies, Plumbing and Heating, Buildings Maintenance and Demolition.

Deirdre Lennox, an immaculate vision of casual beauty many years younger than her husband, greeted her visitor at the front door.

"David, is it? We've been expecting you. Do come in. Want some breakfast?"

He entered, a bit overwhelmed by the opulence of the marble feature hallway adorned with family portraits and was escorted to a conservatory festooned with a huge green array of large exotic plants.

"Find yourself a seat at the table," said Deirdre, "His magnificence will be with you shortly. Excuse me while I fetch the breakfast."

A bemused visitor did as instructed.

It was something of a surprise when Terry Lennox breezed into the room carrying a black coffee, unkempt and unshaven, and dressed in a black vest and shorts, blue slippers and a fluffy white dressing gown. It surprised David because whenever he appeared in public Terry was always very dapper, but on his home turf he was perhaps not the magnificence expected.

The lady of leisure brought a breakfast of Eggs Royale.

"You haven't met my little tribe," Terry slurped and gulped his way through the breakfast, as two youngsters joined them at the table.

"The weirdy beardy is my son Damian. He's hoping to become a tennis professional. Never see him from dawn to dusk, out there practicing on the lawn tennis court I had built for him."

The visitor nodded politely in Damian's direction.

"And then there's the apple of my eye, my lovely daughter Selena. She runs the small beautician's in Crawford Avenue. We just bought her a horse. Haven't we darling?"

David was almost speechless, trying to concentrate on the breakfast, but he felt he ought to say something.

"B-B-But where do keep the horse." he asked clumsily.

"In the paddock behind the outdoor swimming pool. We thought it would be lovely to keep the horse down by the river in Sandersdale." Terry answered nonchalantly as if everybody had all that he had.

Selena looked up and explained, "I call the horse, Missy Clover. She's beautiful, but she has a mind of her own. I could swear she goes into a daydream at times, almost a fantasy world."

"I could feel the luscious warmth of the summer sun on my brown skin, and skipped through the daisy strewn meadow glad to be alive and free. I ambled slowly down to the stream where the waters babbled in an endless hypnotic tune. I took a mouthful of the sweet, cool water, and then laid down under the soothing shade of an old linden tree. I was so glad to be at Sandersdale in a beautiful paddock, with tempting honeyed grass to eat, and a safe, comfy stable."

After breakfast Terry Lennox was remarkably calm when he explained.

"Before you arrived I had a phone call from Tania. She told me that Henry Burrows was found dead at 9 o'clock this morning. Tania said she found him in his office when she returned to collect her umbrella she'd left behind the previous evening. She had stomped out in a huff when Burrows sacked her. At first she thought he was asleep, but he looked so pale, and when she touched his sleeve his body was cold. She said that he was slumped on the ground next to the desk, and there was a lot of Paracetamol strewn across his desk. That's when she called the police and ambulance. It looked like it might be suicide, but the police are investigating due to some "irregularities". Apparently he had been beaten up very severely.

David replied, "Well, he was such a dislikeable person. I wouldn't be at all surprised if someone decided to do him in. Why do you employ such rank arseholes?"

"Well, it's my easy way to do things. I employ obnoxious people to pass on bad news, do the sacking, make redundancies, cut hours and deny pay rises. What Burrows didn't know was that after he'd done all the dirty deeds for me, then he was next for the dole queue. I sacked him over the phone just before he was due to leave the office yesterday evening."

"What! That makes you worse than Burrows."

The boss continued with what looked to David like a worrying nonchalance and a slight grin as if he'd just told an old joke, "It was a brilliant strategy. After he'd sacked everyone else, I phoned him last night at 5.30 and gave him the bullet as well. Looks like he took it badly."

"Is there reasoning behind all this?"

"Yes. The redundancies had to be. You may have heard rumours that Bridges is going bust, and the Bank have threatened to foreclose on my huge mortgage if I don't rationalise my company assets. None of that is true. What's really happening is that I'm breaking into a different area of interest which you may find out about shortly. You know how difficult it is to keep secrets in this town."

"What secrets do you have then Terry?" David enquired cheekily.

Terry just sniggered, gave a strange look and didn't answer.

"What I will tell you is that I'm consolidating my six companies into three. Damsonia Holdings is next to go, then AGFU, and that leaves me with Andersons, Hammonds and Fullmers Demolition."

"Your cunning plans meant that John Wilson, Tania and me were all sacked by Burrows. We look like candidates for his murder."

"Doesn't everybody, including yours truly? Perhaps it would've been easier to bump him off than sack him. He's been a very useful pain in everyone's arse for years, sometimes even in mine."

David was becoming uncomfortable with the casual way in which Terry behaved about the murder.

The Boss said, "The question is, who is the number one suspect?"

David considered the long list of candidates, and then replied, "I'm sure Stuart McPherson will sort it out. He's our local Hercule Poirot."

"Don't make me laugh, Davy Boy. Thirty years in the Fuzz and he's only made Detective Sergeant. I doubt if he could detect an apple in a bag of walnuts."

David's discomfort grew.

"Enough of this morbid talk. I've always appreciated your work ethic and I always fought your corner when Burrows had the hump with you and it's just unlucky that you were employed at Bridges at this difficult time. Now that it's gone tits up, I'd like to offer you a job at Andersons starting Monday if you're interested."

Chapter 8
Saturday 10th November, Evening
Neon Queens

The mobile rang.

"Good evening, Mr. Dimmock, this is the Sanderford and Chilverton Gazette. We have heard from one of your friends that you've recently won the National Lottery. Could we do an interview?"

"No thank you very much."

David ended the call. It rang again 2 minutes later, and the voice on the other end asked exactly the same question. The call was ended in annoyance.

The harassed man began to wonder which one of his "friends" had told the press, but then by now his win was probably common knowledge. It occurred to him that Brenda may have told the Gazette just to create annoyance.

Then the mobile rang again: same number.

It had become a must to avoid any more calls or to risk Brenda/Brian coming back for another battle and so he decided to go out. He took a train for the five minute ride to into Chilverton-on-Sea to go to a night club.

There was a tough guy that nobody wanted to meet in a dark alley slouched on the bar in the Ship's Anchor. He was downing his third vodka, before taking the short walk to The Neon Queens Night Club. He would normally have downed five shorts, but had been a bit late arriving at Chilverton due to a last minute call from Terry Lennox. Soon he made his way along the promenade to his workplace.

There were queues outside the popular venue every night and the ex-boxer played his own game, where he let the girls in, but not their boyfriends. He loved a fight with a lairy, loudmouthed, young upstart. It made his night worthwhile. Lenny Blunden was not his real name. As the club bouncer, he stood outside the entrance door wearing a smug expression that asserted, "Double hard bastard! That's me!" A bald-headed fatso, with hands like bunches of under ripe bananas, he was confident he looked the business in his black jacket, white shirt and bow tie.

"Nobody, but nobody comes in here without my permission." he muttered underneath his breath, as another taxi load of half-drunk Budweiser boys approached him noisily but with a grudging respect.

"Hello Dimmo, long time no see." snarled Lenny Blunden.

David groaned, remembering that he and fatso bouncer had been at Sanderford Grammar together and replied, "Why hello to you, Francis Cockburn or whatever you are calling yourself this week?"

"You know my name you light weight and if you want to come in, then show some respect."

"OK Lenny, you win. Can I come in?"

"Get in the queue and I'll decide after I've dealt with that bunch of pansies." he said, pointing at the Budweiser boys.

"Still letting the juvenile trash into the old glorified disco/bistro then?"

"Keeps the cash registers ticking over for now. That's all going to change soon though. Neon Queens is going upmarket after the takeover. They're looking out for the moneyed gentry. The new owner wants to turn it into a casino."

"Who's the new guy?"

"Can't tell you that, but I can say it might be a well-known local lad with loads of dosh and the right friends to carry it off."

Begrudgingly, Lenny allowed his ex-schoolmate in and David glued himself to the bar, feeling very lonely and wondering why he had ever bothered to come. After an hour of restless boredom, he had become quickly tired of the antics of a crowd of Neanderthal men in a very rowdy stag party and decided to leave. Outside the door of Neon Queens, he encountered Lenny again and noticed how bruised his knuckles were. Lenny knew his old school chum was wondering what happened. He looked at his hands, grinned and said," Had a great time tonight beating up some lairy shithead from Englesfield earlier on. He'll be sucking his breakfast through a straw in the morning."

Out in the cold, David castigated himself, muttering under his breath, "Why did I come here? God, I hate Chilverton, especially in November."

"November, harsh frost, freezing ground,
November, tumbling leaves turning brown,
The Summer now lies fallen,
A cold chill cuts the air,
New season's loom spins out thin snares,
To capture and leave bare.

November, tall flames became a cinder glow,
November, awaits first falls of Winter's snow,
Like echoes in the spells of fate,
Sweet passion staggers in and dies,
November's whims, sly they lie in wait,
To strike their savage, sharp surprise.

November, short days, growing cold,
November, Autumn's secrets to unfold,
With restless soul and sleepless mind,
A candle's flicker flame remains,
The hope for all who fall in love,
Alone, endure a lover's pain."

David leaned himself into the biting wind and fought hard to make some progress along the wide open space of Promenade Avenue, now empty and grey after the neon bright artificial happiness of earlier that night. A stray black cat scurried away frightened, as a dustbin lid flew off and clanging loudly, cart-wheeled along towards a dimly lit shop doorway. Three gentlemen of the road huddled there, shivering in the frosty night air. They battled with each other for the comforting inner glow afforded by the possession of a begrudgingly shared brandy bottle. David turned down a dark narrow alley away from the seafront as a gush of sea air filled his lungs for two seconds. Then, as his feet brushed through piles of discarded paper bearing the familiar scent of vinegar on fish and chips, he could taste the tang of sea salt on his lips. Somewhere in the distance the siren of a police car perforated the steady echoes of angry waves crashing on the beach below.

"Why did I come to this god-forsaken dump?" he asked himself, "I've got to find the station soon and get away from this hell hole."

Station found, and train embarked, he was snug in the warm embrace of the late night train, and in a carriage empty of other passengers, he began to feel the relief of being shut away from the cruel world outside, even if the relief was temporary. His eyes became heavy and he resisted sleep, but the noise and motion of the train had his brain running on overtime.

"You can see nothing,
outside it's dark and black,
but you hear the rhythmic clatter,
of the wheels upon the track,
all surfaces you feel to touch,
are hard, bright and clean,
plastic smell of newness,
inside this mean machine,
international coffee brand,
you taste upon your tongue,
wonder why you came here,
it ain't much fun."

As the train lurched into Sanderford Station, David woke up with a jolt, got off and quickly made his way home. He was relieved to find that neither Brenda nor Brian were indoors. He switched off his mobile and hit the sack.

Chapter 9
Sunday 11th November, Morning
Armistice and Americans

The assembled crowd stood along the green edge of the riverbank close to the town square as the last clang of the eleven o'clock chime echoed from the clock tower outside the Town Hall. Silence fell and everybody stood still; there wasn't a hint of any traffic noise and it seemed that even the birds had stopped singing. For two minutes the only sound that was audible was the lapping of the river waters swirling under the nearby bridge. Then, the silence ended abruptly as a marching band struck the first note of a military tune and began to stride with the neat uniformity of broken time across the bridge towards Willow Tree Park.

David was just coming back from Jeffery's Sunday morning walk and started to cross the town square close to the War Memorial. George was tidying up in the beer garden of the Feathers and issued a cheery wave.

"You OK, Dave? Weather's still pretty good for November, so I'm keeping the beer garden going. Coming in for a pint, mate?"

"No George; got things to do today. See you later."

David turned to walk home, just as a stranger in a check shirt and red baseball cap called out. He was sat with an overdressed woman in a fur coat and Russian hat. They were both drinking halves of Budweiser."

"Hey buddy, spare me a moment,"

"What is it? Can I help you with something?"

"I sure hope so. I'm Chuck Johnson and this is my good lady Darlene. We're on vacation here. We love all your English culture, but wondered why do you have this weirdo celebration in November? It would be great in summer when the sun is shining and it's a bit warmer."

"It's called Armistice Day and it doesn't celebrate; it commemorates all those that died in two world wars, including all your brave G.I.'s."

There were blank looks, indicating that perhaps the only wars the two Americans knew about were in Iraq and Afghanistan.

"We like it here in Olde Englande. Yesterday we had a tour around London on a bus. Saw everything and in the afternoon we went to Windsor. Sure is a great place your little Queenie's got."

David cringed at the inanity and politely asked, "How long are you here?"

"Until tomorrow, when we fly to Scotland. Having a day exploring the mountains in Glasgow and Edinburgh and then we go to Australia."

"Wow! That's a long flight. Do you suffer from jetlag?"

"I don't think so; it's only about 2 hours to Vienna."

David cringed again and smiled generously at the ignorance of these people.

"Have a safe trip. Enjoy yourselves. Nice to have met you."

A few steps along the square David bumped into John Wilson and Mary coming out of St Catherine's Church. John looked terribly haggard and ill at ease, making straight for the pub doorway at the Feathers. Mary stopped to talk.

"John doesn't look at all well." David sympathised.

Mary pulled a sad face and replied, "He hasn't slept for two nights, tossing and turning and mumbling in his sleep. Ever since Thursday he has been pre-occupied, angry and unapproachable, worrying about this situation."

"It must be very difficult for him after thirty years at Bridges."

"I know, but I don't understand why he got so drunk that afternoon and then didn't come home until eight o'clock. George at the Feathers phoned me and told me he'd chucked him out about four."

"I don't know any more than you, because I left about two."

"It's not like him at all. He's normally a very quiet, composed, gentle man."

"But how are you, Mary?"

"I'm OK, we'll get by, somehow: we'll get by." she reflected with a sense of resignation.

"You two have been together for so long, and I don't think anything could split you apart."

"But I'm worried about John. So, he's lost his job. It's a big "So what!" as far as I'm concerned. We've still got a decent income from my job at Flack, Allen and Crosby."

She paused and looked almost apologetically into David's eyes.

"John has taken it so badly, so very badly."

A shift of subject seemed appropriate.

"How was church? Did it help?"

"Reverend Snellgrove gave an interesting sermon for the Armistice Day and spoke very well about the evils of war. But some people in St Catherine's have been giving us terrible looks. Anybody would think that my husband murdered Henry Burrows. I know he was angry and he told me how worked up he had got about it in the Feathers. I can only assume that someone in the pub heard what he said to you and put two and two together and made five. You know how rumours spread in this town."

"Oh Mary, We've worked together at Bridges for many years and I know John's a family man and a good Christian. He doesn't have it in him to hurt people, let alone murder someone."

"Yes, that's so very true. Thank you, David."

They looked at each other searching for something more to add. Nothing came.

"I'd better follow him into the bar, before he gets plastered again," she added half joking.

David continued his homeward trek mulling over the conversation. He truly believed that John had nothing to worry about. It came to him that if anyone wanted to put a contract out on Henry Burrows, then perhaps, Francis Cockburn posing as Lenny Blunden would be the ideal hitman.

Chapter 10
Monday 12th November, Morning
Ashburner

After a quick breakfast on Monday morning, David walked through Magnolia Square and gave a single finger salute to the ghost of Burrows where he would have been at the window of Bridges Construction moaning about the pigeons. Three streets further down the hill and he arrived at Anderson's offices in Cleveland Lane.

It would be hard for him to admit that he was in two minds about it, but he'd decided that he'd just put on a grand act. He wasn't going to let his lottery win burn a hole in his pocket and for the moment, he wasn't going to let it become any more prominent public knowledge that he had close to two million pounds stashed away in the bank. The Sanderford telegraph would soon broadcast his good fortune, but he saw no reason to enlighten anyone personally that didn't have the knowledge. He told himself, *"Carry on as normal and pretend to look for another job while you work out how best to handle your new found wealth."*

His new boss, Mr. Arthur Ashburner was like a pre-pubescent version of Burrows, but instead of the boom of the beast, he had an annoying squeaky voice like a snotty five year old boy whining because he couldn't have his bag of sweets.

"So, you are the poor unfortunate that Mr. Lennox has sent me to help with the accounts?"

It was a question, not a statement, almost as if David didn't know why he was there. Ashburner pointed to an empty and very distressed self-assembly desk, underneath a constantly flickering ceiling light. He dumped a large mound of papers in front of his new recruit and without any guidance whatsoever, nodded to indicate that he should start sorting them out immediately.

"Let's get started!" he droned and the new boy already began to wonder how many other "assistants" had passed through his office and lasted less than a day. He took off his jacket and studied the first invoice, but he needed Arthur to explain how things were supposed to work at Andersons Holdings. He gave it back to him and asked a few questions. He got no help, just an exasperated look, before it was taken, or should it be snatched back, with the irritating little Hitler youth candidate whining, "For Heaven's sake man, don't you know what to do?" Then he puffed out his cheeks and added, "OK! I suppose I'll have to do it."

After a few minutes, it appeared to David, that the Anderson's accountant had even more similarities to Henry Burrows. The central heating was turned up to an uncomfortable maximum, but Arthur remained happily sweating in his thirty year old, blue pin striped, "Man at C & A" suit. The "hand it back to me" process was repeated over and over again, until the apprentice's desk was clear and the Boss was piled high with work to do. There was good reason.

Ashburner didn't want an assistant. He was an old school one man band. He was probably thinking, *"Yippee! Its monthly accounts and I love columns of figures. I've been here for 29 years and nobody does it better. There is absolutely no way that some snotty faced jumped up whizz kid with a CIPFA is taking any part of this job away from me."*

After twiddling his mathematical thumbs for a while, staring into space, the reluctant apprentice put his jacket back on and said a polite, "Goodbye, Mr. Ashburner."

He got out of there as quick as a ferret in a rabbit burrow. Outside, he took out his mobile and called Terry Lennox, telling him that he had resigned after less than an hour. Terry made out, not very convincingly, that he was sorry and persuaded David to meet him at the Feathers at seven that evening.

Chapter 11
Monday 12th November, Evening
A Bend in the Road?

David was feeling a bit pissed off and not at all keen on going out. Jeffery was sat on his lap fast asleep with his little legs up in the air. The telly was illustrating the usual soporific garbage.

"Oh well." he said to himself, "I suppose I'd better find out what Mr. Big wants from me. I hope it's not another offer of an Ashburner experience."

It was a short but brisk walk from Newcastle Gardens to The Feathers, as it was bitter cold with an unrelenting biting wind. Rushing along, David was glad to soon be in the warmth of the olde worlde former coaching inn. He spotted Terry Lennox in the cosy corner next to the open fire, talking to Peter Thornton in what looked like a very heated argument. As soon as he arrived the discussion stopped like a train running into the buffers and for a moment, both men looked uncomfortably in David's direction.

"Davy boy! Good of you to come. Can I get you a pint? Old Rustic Nectar isn't it?"

Terry went to the bar and Peter just sat motionless silently staring at the fruit machine. When Mr. Big returned, slopping along, armed with two pints, he sat back down, took a large swig of bitter and poured a Jaegerbomb into the glass. Peter waved cursorily at the two men and without a sound, quickly exited the pub.

"OK, Davy, I'm glad you've come for a chat. We've got a lot of things to discuss. First of all about you being sacked by Burrows."

"Am I meant to be grateful for being sacked?" David interrupted indignantly.

Terry pulled an irritated expression, rolled his eyeballs and stared briefly at the ceiling. Then he replied, "Let's put it this way Davy boy. There have been a few ups and downs in the last week for you."

David hated being called Davy boy and grimaced before he answered.

"How do you mean?"

"Well, I think you'll agree that there was an enormous "Up" when you won the lottery?"

"That's true."

"But things went downhill when Brenda left you."

David smiled and sipped at his beer.

"In the end I might regard that differently."

"How's that?"

"Let's just say that it's definitely going to be an "Up" in the end."

"I'm not going to ask for any detail, but I know what you mean about Brenda. It's no secret that I never had much time for the moaning bitch."

"And the feeling eventually became mutual. It took a while to learn what a cow she is."

The chat was interrupted by an uncomfortable silence as both men collected their thoughts. David wondered where the conversation might be leading next.

Terry broke the ice, "Admittedly there was a "Down" when Burrows sacked you."

"Didn't you do that indirectly though?"

"I suppose I did, but I always had something else in mind for you."

"Really! I'm all ears." was the reply, with an undisguised note of sarcasm.

Terry gulped at his beer and pulled a face to imply that he didn't much enjoy the taste of Old Rustic Nectar Premium with a Jaegerbomb. He was obviously only drinking it for a therapeutic, or was it anaesthetic, effect. The glass went down on the table and he looked at David wide eyed and certain of himself.

"Well, what you need to know is that I was always looking out for you at Bridges. Burrows was never that keen on you and I sorted him out from time to time to make sure you were able to stay there."

"And right now I am meant to be grateful again for that and for being sacked?" A reply even more indignant.

Terry held up his hand and pleaded, "Hold on there, Davy boy."

"Look Terry, don't call me Davy boy and let's cut to the chase. Where exactly is all this leading?"

"OK, here's the reason why I wanted to meet you here tonight. I have two job offers on the table for your consideration."

"What have you got in mind for someone who honestly doesn't give a shit? I'm well covered with my lottery win and I intend to fully enjoy it."

Ignoring the impatience Mr. Big smiled, got up, went to the bar and soon returned with two more pints.

"Don't be like that. I think you might be interested to hear what I've got to say."

There was an awkward pause as David remained silent, sipping at his beer and Terry quaffed a huge gulp. It was obvious by now that he'd had quite a few.

Mr. Big was slurring his words as he said, "I've just been talking to Peter. He's going to be looking after all my building firms while I concentrate on my new project. I've decided it's time to diversify. So I'm taking over Neon Queens, going to refurbish the place and take it up market. Perhaps it will end up as a casino."

"So, what's that got to do with me?"

"I'm offering you two possible jobs. Either to be Peter's Assistant Manager helping to run the buildings operations or to invest in the night club and become my partner."

Immediate thoughts were, *"No more buildings jobs, thank you."* followed by, *"I see, so I'm now a prime candidate to be touched for loads of dosh because I've won the lottery."*

Another pint and another Jaegerbomb were on the verge of being demolished.

"Have another drink."

"Not for me, thank you, I've hardly started on this pint."

Terry went back to the bar and came back with a refill and then through the slurring and slurping, he then tried to wax philosophical.

"The way I look at it is like this."

Another gulp of beer.

"If there's a bend in the road ahead, maybe all your fair-weather friends will only see the end of the road. But remember that a bend in the road is not the end of the road, it is just a change of direction."

"I think I've said all I needed to say." came the reply. David wasn't going to be persuaded to consider either offer.

"So have I." was the return. Terry didn't have the composure to do any persuading.

There was silence and within seconds, Terry drained his glass and picked up his mobile. He had decided to call Arnie up and go home.

By the time the chauffeur arrived, his boss was on the verge of collapsing. He was helped out to the Rolls by the two men. Arnie gave a look as if to say, "Not again!" as the two of them slumped the drunkard on to the back seat.

"Been drinking shots in the bitter again, I suppose. Anyway, hop in and I'll take you home after dropping him off."

There was some reluctance to take the offer, but the icy rain was a convincer.

The journey to Sandersdale House was almost over when the passenger rose from his stupor and promptly puked explosively out of the window. Then, for one slightly more coherent moment, he revived enough to slur, "By the way, I'm taking the boat out for a little trip in the morning. Get yourself over to Cullington Quay at eight tomorrow. Bring Jeffery if you wish. You've got an invitation to a booze cruise, Davy boy."

They dragged him into the mansion and positioned him in an

armchair in the lounge. Arnie moaned, "That has happened twice a week, every week, for the past few months. Look! He'll be furious if I don't get him a gallon of coffee and scrape him up off the floor. Sorry, but I can't take you home, unless you can wait about an hour or so."

David walked home through an extremely violent thunderstorm, determined not to take up the booze cruise invitation.

Chapter 12
Wednesday14th November, Evening
Moving fingers write

It had been nearly a week since he had won the lottery and David was sure that by now, everyone knew about it. Sanderford was a small town and everybody knew everyone else and usually all their business. So when he arrived at the Library in the Oscar Wilde Hall on the town square for his monthly writer's group meeting, the gang were all there with two subjects on their minds. They all wanted to know what he intended to do following the lottery win, being sacked by Bridges and having Brenda walk out on him. That was a poor second behind the demise of Henry Burrows. Sanderford certainly wasn't like the fictional TV village of Midsomer. There weren't many crimes committed, let alone murders. The most outrageous misdemeanors were more likely to be, either being back late with your library books or, heaven forbid, parking on a double yellow line.

However, the group leader, Peter Thornton decided to curtail all discussion until the tea break, usually midway through the meeting, so that everyone would have a chance to read their latest piece of writing without distraction. It appealed greatly to his need to be in charge.

"I'm going to ban all discussion of the death of Henry Burrows until I decide the time is right to talk about it. Murder," he quickly corrected himself, "Or is it suicide? Are two very complicated issues. While we are at it, I don't want any talk about our young friend's good fortune either. This is a writing group, not the social services."

Peter Thornton was a control freak who worked for Terry Lennox and enjoyed his prominent position as his Mr. Fixit. It was common knowledge that he hated Henry Burrows with a vengeance, so although it might be a longshot, he may have been a possible suspect for the murder.

Peter was very well read, but unfortunately, he was a tubby, balding pretentious prat with a goatee beard. He always knew a better way to describe anything and everything. He wanted to be a famous author and persistently advised his group, "Dickens would say it like this." or, "C S Lewis would write the story something more like that." Unfortunately for him, he never practiced what he preached.

He had an annoying habit of starting his readings with an unnecessary and often irrelevant preamble just to show all his "pupils" how clever he was. There was no doubt that he had always prepared in advance and practiced what he was going to say before he started reading his contribution.

"I write these words in the fervent hope that I am forever remembered in the stardust that holds the secrets of the Universe and not in the rancid box that holds the dregs of civilisation in a cesspit under an ancient railway arch."

Nearly all present were thinking, "Oh well! There he goes again. What in Heaven's name is he on about?"

There was no point in reacting. He wouldn't listen anyway. Following that irritating introduction, he read something proselytizing, calling it "Fame, fortune and fulfillment!" (Yes! He loved exclamation marks).

Before his reading, he handed round copies of his latest effort.

"There are many options for achieving fame, fortune and fulfillment.

You can jump over the gate that guards the backyard to fame.

You can walk boldly up to the enormous front door and bulldoze or smash it down. If you want the famous future, you can go up and smash in the door, but you may discover that your pleasure will be short-lived

You can ring the bell and wait patiently 'til someone answers and ask politely to be let in.

Ask yourself, "What do you want fame for?"

Is it for its own sake or for the future that it may bring? If you want fame for its own sake, for the accompanying adulation, then you can sneak in the back gate. Your stealth may be temporarily rewarded, but you may tire of the adulation.

The pursuit of fortune may be futile or it may drop into your lap unexpectedly. Whatever! It will surely make you infamous rather than famous and any fulfillment derived from it may be temporary.

Or do you want to be fulfilled in that something which you have been talented enough to create and to offer that freely to others? If you want to be fulfilled, then go up quietly, ring the bell and ask to be let in. Use your talents in a humble way. They are gifts that you did not develop alone. Remember all those that planted your seed and then helped you water that seed to grow your talent. You may continue to grow and to give as long as you are not distracted and diverted by the twin temptations of fame and fortune. Use your gifts wisely, so that you may continue to grow and to give."

It was more like a lecture or a sermon, but that was the way Peter did it. Reactions were always a bit terse, despite the group's terms of reference.

"The Writing Group was formed with the purpose of sharing experiences of writing in an informal social gathering and to continue to, collectively and independently, develop our individual writing skills. In short, to help each other to become better at writing. We all hoped that members of the group would enrich the process by bringing back their work and illustrating the processes by which it was created and hopefully brought to publication."

"Very good!" said John Wilson nervously, but then all present knew that for some reason, John appeared to be scared of Peter, so they expected that he wouldn't in any way critique his work. It was noticeable that John, who was usually calm and collected, was more on edge than his fellow writers were used to.

"Yes, I agree, a good examination of fame, fortune and fulfillment. Liked your introduction as well." was an, as usual, patronising comment from Stuart McPherson. He and Peter had known each other since their schooldays.

David thought that the group leader was getting too much praise or maybe too little critique, so he offered, "Do you want to be famous, accrue a fortune or earn fulfillment then? Because you can have one, two or all three of them."

Then he added, carefully trying to deflect attention from his recent good fortune, which he knew by now would be one of the major news items in town. "Even though most of us don't acquire any of them, personally I'd like fulfillment."

"That's easy for you to say," came the speedy reply, "Now that you've joined the millionaire club. What's more, you did it without any effort other than spending a few quid on a lottery ticket. You didn't have to work for that, did you?"

"No, but I had to wait for it, and paradoxically until the time that I got the bum's rush from my job. I wonder what part you played in that?"

Peter ignored the question. "If you read my offering carefully, you will see that what I am saying is that you can get any of the three in many different ways It could be fame by winning X-Factor or committing a heinous crime. It could be fortune by working at it like Terry Lennox or Mr. Lucky Git, by winning the lottery like you did. Then there's fulfillment by being good at something and getting noticed. What I want is fulfillment." Peter explained, lying through his teeth.

Frank Archer interrupted, "Come on boys, play nice. This is supposed to be a social group. We shouldn't be talking about whether we want fame, fortune or fulfillment, but about Peter's writing. I think it's a fair assessment, written well and gives a lot of food for thought."

"Thank you, Frank." said Peter with a sickly smile.

"Let's move on. What have you got for us John?"

The token lady present, "Davina" Middleton, wasn't too bothered about offering any comment. As usual, she spent half her time at the meeting on her mobile, contacting friends on Facebook. She was always pre-occupied, but that evening for some reason, she was also very on edge. Sometimes, the others doubted that she listened to anybody else's written pieces.

John cleared his throat, explained that he had two short poems to offer and read the first of his latest pieces of philosophical prose.

"Forbidden fruit can only be found,
in a secret garden close to the ground.
Watered by new wine, not watered by rain,
picked by hand at the essence of ripeness."

"Shadows are always there. What do they say?
Sunshine comes and goes from day to day.
There are distant rainbows painted on the sky
while sun and rain run busy passing by
But there's nothing cools the blood and fills the dread,
as angry thunder and lightning overhead.
Swift justice meted out, Oh so sweet revenge,
Hell to all my foes, Heaven to my friends."

Without waiting for a reaction, he then read the second piece.

"If you are going to build bridges over a raging stream, then
you must be prepared to be the first to walk across them
If you weather the storm, tossed and torn,
if you set fire to the wheel,
if you desire to make a deal,
if you steal a furtive glance,
if you get a second chance,
if you turn over a new leaf,
are prepared to die for your beliefs,
Perhaps too tired to be inspired.
if you can keep your dreams alive,
then by chance you may survive."

John looked up contented and anticipated a favourable response.

Peter was first with a nasty question, "Did you write those before or after you got pissed in the Feathers last Thursday?"

"I scribbled up both of those since last Thursday, as I've had a bit of time on my hands, due to unforeseen circumstances." John replied, irritated, and staring angrily at the questioner.

"Nice words. Liked the second one best." said Frank, breaking the tension. "The first one seemed to about revenge."

"OK! It's not Byron or Shelley, but well done." contributed Peter begrudgingly.

"I found the 'bridges over a raging stream very interesting' and I thought the bit where you repeated the use of the seven words a line from where you say, "If you set fire to the wheel", grabbed attention very effectively." was the constructive offering from David.

"Don't really get philosophy," admitted Davina, finding a moment to break off from her Facebook obsession and shuffling uncomfortably in her seat, "It's a bit too deep for me."

"I'm OK with it." Stuart said, "Makes you think about yourself and the way you live your life. It's got good imagery like building bridges over a raging stream, weathering the storm, tossed and torn, keeping your dreams alive, dying for your beliefs. We all have burdens to carry around. Life and death and surviving through trials and tribulations; isn't that really what it's all about?"

Chapter 13
Wednesday 14th November, Evening
Having writ, moves on

Stuart McPherson was the next to contribute. He was a friend of Peter, tall, gangly and old before his time, with very pretty wife and no kids. He was at the writer's group attempting to write a crime novel, of which there had been very little evidence so far. As a Detective Sergeant, now close to early retirement, he was perhaps looking for one last significant job and hoping to get assigned to the Burrows case. To some pccasionally there was something a little worrying about his behaviour with anybody in the village. Many suspected, in the nicest possible way, he spread himself around a whole range of local events and meetings just to spy on people, but the last thing he was likely to be was a poor and rather obvious henchman for the Gestapo. He was a nice respectable and largely well-respected citizen of Sanderford. However, this particular Wednesday, his presence had been a little unsettling as it was fairly obvious that he had studied faces and mannerisms intently, and looking for clues that might assist with the murder investigation.

"Sorry, we've been far too busy recently with the local crime busters trying to figure out who the guilty culprit is for you-know-who's murder. Haven't had time to put anything together."

"No change there then." thought David, with knowing looks from John and Frank.

Next to read was "Davina" Middleton. She was the stereotype lesbian with a closely shaved head, a multitude of tattoos on her bare and podgy arms and piercings in her nose and eyebrows. It had always come as something of a surprise to everyone to learn that she was Tania's sister, because she was the complete opposite in attitude and appearance. Snotty, fractious and belligerent were her best characteristics. Her real name was Sharon Thompson. She was a close friend of David's wife, Brenda and had recently "converted" from being bi-sexual.

As an avid reader of Barbara Cartland, she consequently indulged in writing what might be termed sexy romances. The only trouble was, especially in this all-male forum, they were a bit too sexy, mainly because she was so obviously obsessed with blowjobs. She smiled, and they all prepared to listen politely, but knew where the story would eventually travel to.

"A few days ago, Richard and Alice had given their vows in a wonderful ceremony at St Margaret's, a Saxon church on the outskirts of the village of Great Potterton. When they left in rapture for their honeymoon, they could not divert their eyes from each other's loving gaze. They arrived in France, smiling and laughing in the magic of a secluded Alpine valley, to spend a week in their hideaway chalet within view of Mont Blanc. The warm glow of moonlight shimmered on Alice's soft, pale skin and her sparkling green eyes swallowed Richard again. That night they knew they would hold each other so close and tremble to the dancing rhythm of their love, echoing through the night like a gypsy violin. Their lips brushed and in that moment they stood alone.

"You are mine. "He whispered.

All was silence, peace, serenity, and loving eyes gazed across the room at Richard. Alice's beautiful auburn hair flowed gently across her shoulders, framing a face lit up with longing. Two hearts thumped and breathing quickened. Then a haunting sound surrounded the two of them, swirling around them like crashing boulders. Bells rang, horns sounded, and they fixed eyes again, lost for words. Tenderly their lips met, tongues began searching. In that moment they closed their eyes in blissful rapture.

Richard's thought were, "She's mine now."

Alice said to herself, "He's with me at last."

A sense of security and warmth surged through their bodies, as they passed the point of no return and began to tear at each other's clothes......."

David noticed that John was yawning and Peter was staring out of the window. He switched off at that point. It's one of Sharon's "romances". Everyone in the club knew that it was time for the graphically descriptive blowjob. Davina carried on regardless. All the gentlemen present were relieved when it was over.

"Very romantic," offered Peter, "But I think we've heard it before."

"Especially the bit about the blowjob." thought David.

"Never liked romantic novels and never will." admitted Frank, adding, "In particular, this one that you keep regurgitating every month."

John appeared to be far away, but then woke up with a start and feeling he ought to comment, he caused a ripple of embarrassment when he said, "Reminded me of when Mary and I first got together."

Then he swiftly added, "Until you got to the rude bit. Not badly written, I suppose."

Davina didn't care what criticism or praise she achieved. She lived in her own very strange world. Every man present wanted to move on quickly from another slightly embarrassing episode of "The Blowjob Chronicles".

It was now Frank Archer's turn to read and true to form, he covered very similar ground to the previous month. He was the old git, dull and lacking confidence, a failure, salt and pepper moustache and beard, married with 5 kids and a massive mortgage, who couldn't wean himself away from his miserable time in military service, even though he hated every minute of it. Frank was a dullard who worked for Sanderford Council in the Planning Department. Nobody had ever met his wife and they all wondered what she had ever seen in him. Unfortunately his time in the army was the only significant thing he had done in his long and boring life. He sat there, ram rod back straight as if he was a sergeant major in his new uniform of brown corduroy trousers, check shirt and brown shoes with all the expectation of a fast asleep sloth. To humour him was the best policy; otherwise he would get very sullen and fail to contribute anything to the remainder of the meeting.

"My God, why must he only write about military things if he hated being in the army so much?" thought Peter.

"Please! Don't mention the war!" thought David.

Davina said nothing and thought about her next episode of "Everyone loves a blowjob!"

Frank began, "I've got two poems about the same subject and very relevant, as we've just commemorated Armistice Day last Sunday. The first is called, "Armistice". Then he read:

My boy's years behind me, once eager and bold,
For King and for Country, for freedom I'm told,
Kitchener wants me, with courage inspired,
To beat down the Kaiser, and save the Empire.

We marched off to war, patriotic and proud,
Girls cheered and threw flowers, bands played long and loud,
But excitement soon done, the ugly truth dawned;
For battle in Flanders, unlearned and unwarned.

In waterlogged trenches, all barbed wire and mud,
Machines guns and mustard gas, wasted our blood,
Deafened and deadened, and shell-shocked and spent,
As four years of comrades in arms came and went.

In safety remote great Generals planned,
Sacrifices relentless for acres of land,
At Ypres and Verdun and along the Somme,
In savage abandon, shells, bullets and bombs.

Then orders came down, "Attack! Boys Attack!"
As dark stench of death hung heavy and black,
And choking back tears, with no chance for Goodbyes,
I watched helpless as brave men were blown to the skies.

All the King's horses and all the King's men,
Couldn't patch Charlie together again,
In my pocket his diary to give to his wife,
Not much to show for such a young life.

Today there's a strange eerie sense in the air,
There's rumours an armistice has been declared,
Have the Germans surrendered? Have we won victory?
Is it over for good, or just temporary?

So they've worked out a truce timed precise to the minute,
A ceasefire dreamed up by a war-monger cynic,
In some mad numbers game eleven was chosen,
Fate marched to that standstill. The instant was frozen.

Though sadder and wiser we came home as men,
A land fit for heroes they promised us then,
A fast fading band who fought a lost cause,
now remembers the War an end to all wars."

Frank didn't bother to look up before he went on, "I've written another one, same theme and it's got two alternative titles, either "Ghost of a Ploughman", or "Fair Poppy Fields of France", whichever takes your fancy."

When jingoism swayed me to patriotic fervour,
And posters so ubiquitous drove enthusiasm further,

Kitchener's pointing finger declared the Empire surely needs me,
I signed up quick, and agreed to go where King and Country lead me,
To be on the side of victory and justice for my God,
Not an unknown soldier in a lonely cemetery, a piece of cannon fodder.

Then the noises of battle flooded my ears,
Like an avalanche in my head,
And surrounded me with blood-curdling screams,
From the dying and the dead,
And the air was so foul, like breathing soup,
Bursting my lungs like the devil's embrace,
While the ripping hail sought to impale me,
Like shards of glass on my face.

Then every trench had the stench of death,
From battered, bitter corpses,
While every man fought for every breath,
Among dismembered, bloated horses,
I was tramping in my trench foot boots,
In the mud, and the blood, and skinny starving rats,
There was only one exit from this hell,
And it's not shown on the general's maps.

When the last whistle blew we flew over the top,
Brothers in arms, and yet we all know,
Kitchener's a lying, warmongering bastard,
Now why did we say we would go?
Oh Yes! We were persuaded to join up,
When they led all our boys a merry old dance,
And all we are now are the ghosts of a ploughman,
In the fair poppy fields of France."

Despite his obsession, all the assembled listeners had to concede that Frank wrote very good emotion filled poems.

"I like them both! They are very contemporary and put you right in the trenches in that terrible, terrible conflict that wasted so many young lives." John contributed.

"The poems don't have that special essence of Robert Laurence Binyon's poem "For the Fallen", but they're pretty moving." admitted Peter grudgingly.

"I think it's bloody brilliant to evoke memories from something that happened over a hundred years ago," said David, "Well done!"

Davina said nothing as it was impossible for her to comprehend anything so deeply ancient and reminiscent of a more difficult time.

"Thank you for your encouragement, gentlemen." Frank replied.

Time had been racing on rapidly and all present began to wonder whether the master of ceremonies was going to allow any discussion of the major subjects of the day. Seat shuffling and fidgety glances at wrist watches filled the room. Peter sensed reluctantly that it was time to call a break.

Chapter 14
Wednesday 14th November, Evening
Writing is on the wall

"So, what are you going to do with your ill-gotten gains?" snarled Peter.

Ignoring the attitude, David quietly replied, "Oh, do a bit of travelling, see the world and when I come back, buy myself a nice new house."

"In Sanderford, I hope." queried John.

"Wouldn't want to live anywhere else, John." came the reply.

"Well, my friend, I wish you the best of luck."

There were somewhat begrudging nods for the rest of the crew except for Peter.

"That's quite enough of that," said Peter, "Let's move on."

There was a heavy silence prompted by the obvious mood of jealousy exhibited in Herr Obersturmbann Fuhrer cutting short the discussion. All, except one present, smiled a knowing smile at David. Only Davina failed to react, feverishly Facebooking away.

"Well, I suppose the next subject will be the unfortunate demise of Henry Burrows?" asked Peter, barely disguising a telltale smirk.

"Mr. Nasty, he got what was coming to him." John offered assertively.

"A thoroughly deserved ending for an obnoxious bully." interjected Peter.

"OK, don't keep on about the bleedin' obvious," Stuart instructed, "We all know what he was like. Nevertheless, we need to know what happened."

"We don't know what happened, do we?" was the unexpected retort from Davina.

"To be quite frank, we don't know yet. At first it looked like suicide, but there are some irregularities I can't tell you about at the moment. He had some injuries and it appears the attack on him was, shall we say, mob-handed."

"Well I suppose that's me, Tania and John are in the frame after he'd sacked us all earlier that day?" David questioned.

"It's likely you will be called in to help us with our enquiries. When all said and done, you all have a motive in that he sacked you that very afternoon."

"That's a ridiculous assumption," asserted David, "Nobody ever killed someone because they were sacked; and how could Tania have murdered him? You're in a fantasy world there, Stuart."

"Nevertheless," he said, "Nevertheless."

After far too long, in Peter's eyes, the discussion about David's lottery win and Henry Burrows murder began to grind to an unsatisfactory conclusion.

It was then David's turn to present a short piece of work about his favourite golfer. He had decided to walk in his shoes by writing in the first person.

"Effortlessly I stride along with my head brushing the clouds of a mile-high sky. I hear the wild cheering of a vast beaming crowd growing louder and louder as I near the last obstacle, only a few hundred yards from the point where I started to walk. My hand is held high in gratitude, and I turn towards the sea of faces, to my right, to my left, repeating the sequence. Smiling incessantly I salute their praise by touching the peak of my cap as the warmth of the July sunshine enfolds me in a welcome glow.

"It doesn't get much better than this.", I tell myself, as I stop and take a long, deep, cool breath, to compose myself for the final small effort.

"Just one more simple action and the job is nearly completed."

The excited crowd is now hushed, motionless, not daring to breathe as if frozen in time, each individual silently urging me on. Through the overwhelming silence I could sense my heart beating as I took a swing, and the ball popped up from the turf, flew over a deep sand bunker, bumped over a small low ridge, landed on the sacred green, and rolled and rolled and rolled. Nearer and nearer to the hole it ran, and with the cheers rising to a crescendo like someone turning up the sound on a radio, I still heard that wonderful reassuring sound as the ball fell into the cup with that characteristic satisfying plop. Now I was truly ecstatic; the happiest man in England. My face ached with the spontaneous easy effort of the biggest, widest smile in the world. Then I could feel my eyes filling up as I cried unashamedly."

"What's that all about?" asked Peter.

"I put myself in the shoes of Justin Rose as he completed his final round in the Open Golf Championship at Royal Birkdale in July 1998."

"Do you play golf?"

"Yes!"

"Do you love it?"

"Maybe! But not as much as I love the music of Bob Dylan, so I also wrote this last week."

"A face that is young but says "I know!" framed by a shock of unkempt dark hair, stares with hollow, fixed eyes through me. His mouth is set in an attitude that is half smile and half sneer, and his body language says, "Why have you dared to interrupt me?"

He is arrogant, but not aggressive. This man is the guru of a generation, love him or hate him his existence and influence cannot be denied. Who else but he would have had the confidence, the talent, the brass-necked cheek, to do what he set out to do? With the relentless passage of time he still reminds me with every irreverent phrase, gesture, posture, of a bygone era when one could truly say, "The times they are a-changing"

Who is it? Why! Bob Dylan, of course."

"Dylan can't sing." Peter argued, "He's just a nasal drone and he's boring."

David smiled, more in exasperation than delight, and answered, "I doubt if you have ever read the words to Mr. Tambourine Man or listened to Dylan singing Blind Willie McTell."

"What's that got to do with it?"

David sighed, "The answer is, obviously not."

After a few seconds contemplation, David decided that he had suffered enough. It came to him that in the last few days, many boats had been burned and this was just another that needed a small spark to burst satisfactorily into flames. It was time to tell it like it is, albeit with something of a tongue in cheek twist and a little mischief. He looked Peter in the eyes with an unusually real assertiveness and pronounced.

"So, Peter, unlike you I am not very well read, but I tried to read all the recommended books. It was too much like hard work. George Orwell was alright if you have a messy suicide in mind, but Leonard Cohen does it better. Perhaps it would have been better if that boring old fart Thomas Hardy had been literate and then he might have been able to write proper English. What the Dickens was Charlie boy trying to tell us? His stories were good, but he always used a hundred words to describe anything where twenty would have sufficed. His books make bloody good door stops."

Peter was not used to this brand of somebody's raw truth from anyone, let alone David. His words would not come. "But, But, But...."

"Someone told me that old Wilfred Shakespeare was an alcoholic manic depressive and he bought all his stuff from a bloke in a pub called Francis Bacon, (that's the bloke, not the pub!), for few pints of lager. I heard that the Bronte sisters made bloody good scones. Not for me, all this classics nonsense. No! Give me something that rhymes, has rhythm and meter and purpose and tells a story in a few minutes, preferably something that can also be set to music. I honestly think that Spike Milligan's Puckoon was the best book ever written and by the way did you know that Roald Dahl's real name was Ronald Dahlia, but he changed it so that people didn't think he was gay."

Peter's face showed a mask of horror at the irreverence of what was David's amusing take on famous authors. Everyone else just quietly smiled and thought, *"It's about time that pretentious prat got his rude awakening."*

What this had all been leading up to was the recent lottery winner issuing a goodbye, "I've decided to quit this little gathering. I wish you all good luck with your attempts at writing."

He thought about awarding a parting shot for everyone before he got up and left, but decided to keep it to himself."

"Peter, you can't teach an old dog new tricks, but you love to teach old tricks to a new dog. You are beyond a shadow of a doubt Mr. Cliché.

John, you have my sympathy because you are basically a very nice bloke who has always deserved a better deal in life. Unfortunately, I am certain that if the sun shone out of your behind, then you would still be inclined to burn your arse.

Stuart, were you ever a detective? Thank God that soon the police force will soon no longer need to depend upon your detective work. Maybe somewhere in the depths of your character there lurks an Hercule Poirot, but I'm not sure that you know how to activate him.

Sharon, Davina or whatever you are calling yourself this week, I've listened to your stories for a long time and I am perplexed. Why do all your stories have to finish with Captain Pugwash and his mate Seaman Staines?

Frank, has anyone ever told you that the war was over long ago? Why can't you move on and cover something cheerful and uplifting?

All of you, if you don't like my scribbles, I don't care. Just as every dog shall have his day, every day shall have its dog. And in literature terms you've all had your day, and I am set to be top dog. Farewell!"

David went home to Jeffery.

Chapter 15
Thursday 15th November, Morning
The Gazette

SANDERFORD AND CHILVERTON GAZETTE

Issue: n20 - 46   15th November, 2020

++

===

Suicide or Murder?

Henry Burrows, the General Manager of Bridges Property Services was found dead at his office in Magnolia Square, Sanderford on the morning of Friday 9th November.

Earlier reports indicated that he had committed suicide, but after further investigation, it was revealed that he had sustained a number of serious injuries.

The Detective Inspector leading the investigation has told us in a press statement that, "The police are looking at a wide range of different possibilities for how Mr. Burrows met his unfortunate demise."

Terry Lennox, well-known local businessman and owner of Bridges told the Gazette, "I have known Henry for over 20 years as a work colleague and a friend. He was a keen golfer and had won the Sanderford Open in July this year. "

The death comes after a rumour that Bridges Property Services was sold to a local buildings consortium for an undisclosed sum on Thursday 8th November and resulted in a series of redundancies for long term staff. Mr. Lennox declined to give any further comment or to offer any more detail concerning the takeover.

Mr. Burrows leaves an estranged wife Daphne and a 17 year old daughter Vivienne, who was recently admitted to Bunington Hospital Psychiatric Unit after frequent arrests for violent behaviour.

Chapter 16
Thursday 15th November, Afternoon
Private Investigations

Stuart had finished reading the short newspaper report in the Sanderford and Chilverton Gazette and reflected on how consistently the paper would get things wrong.

"Why can't they ever get their facts right. Bridges Construction and Planning, not Bridges Property Services. An 18 year old son, Vivian, not a 17 year old daughter, Vivienne. Why don't they check their facts more thoroughly?"

He poured himself a drink and sat down, thinking about how hard done by as a detective he was. Nevertheless he was determined to right some wrongs if assigned to the Burrows murder case.

"Just because I'm only Detective Sergeant Stuart McPherson doesn't mean I'm not a bloody good detective. So, I didn't get promoted to Detective Inspector even after all those years in the force. Right at the beginning they told me "Nice guys don't cut ice in this job. You've got to have an edge, a bit of a nasty streak." But they were always very quick to bring me in on jobs where I could play the Mr. Nice and someone else would play the Mr. Nasty, it's that "Good Cop, Bad Cop" thing. And guess who always got the credit when the suspect was nailed? Not me, not good old Stuart. I've never stopped doing my bit in Sanderford to carefully snoop and stare and listen to everyone around me, to be suspicious and alert and diligent. Well now I'm looking forward to retiring, I'll show them all who is the premier gumshoe round here. I'm going to solve this Henry Burrows murder mystery. See if I don't."

He sat back in his armchair with a vodka and tonic, and his detective's notebook, feeling very confident. The one thing that he was so sure of in being a copper in Sanderford was that he was very good at keeping his ears and his eyes open. He was certain that people respected him and saw him as a friendly policeman. He was no Stasi sniffer dog, there to snitch on anybody who stepped out of line, but he knew everybody well enough to have acquired his personal character references for all of them. He sipped at the vodka, added some more tonic and began to assess the situation, thinking out loud.

"Let's look at the information so far. So! Nobody will be crying in their beer about the murder of Henry Burrows. He was a thoroughly unlikeable, even distasteful character. He delighted in making people feel uncomfortable and he didn't give a damn about upsetting them. That gives plenty of scope to work out who might have wanted to sort him out. But who would want to take things as far as murder?"

He stared into space for a few moments before he began to collect his thoughts on possible suspects. Thinking out loud again.

"It seems to be well established that Burrows met his demise some time during the evening of Friday 9th November. Earlier in the day, he had set about a process of sacking his staff. David Dimmock, John Wilson and Tania Thompson were the victims of this purge, the reasons for which are currently unknown. The company, Bridges Construction, was owned by Terry Lennox and Burrows had been in charge there for more than 14 years. We need to interview Terry Lennox first. He is Mr Big in this town and pulls all the strings there are to be pulled. There has to be a good reason he wants to sack the workers."

He stopped for a bit of reflection on what was happening at Bridges.

"If Lennox was closing Bridges down, he would also have sacked Burrows. I wouldn't be surprised if Lennox hatched a plan to get Burrows to sack everybody and after he'd done the dirty work, to then sack him as well. Yeah, that's very likely. Got to interview Terry Lennox to find out the truth."

He got up from his armchair and went to the sideboard. He replenished his vodka and tonic and sat back down. He reassured himself.

"Everybody knows what a nasty piece of work Burrows was and therefore he will have many enemies. But exactly why was he murdered and who did it? What do we know so far?"

A pause, for collecting thoughts, and then told himself.

"Burrows was found dead in the Bridges office at 9 o'clock on the morning of 9th November by Tania Thompson. Apparently he was slumped on the ground next to the desk and there were some Paracetamol strewn across the desk and floor. She called the police and ambulance. It looked like it might be suicide, but further investigations are required due to some irregularities. It seems he has been the victim of a very violent assault and has a whole range of injuries. Precisely what is not clear at the moment and we'll have to wait for the Crime Scene Investigation reports.

Need to talk to Tania, but there is no way she could murder anyone. She's such a nice, respectable girl and would be more likely to cry in a corner than hurt anybody after being sacked.

David Dimmock was also sacked and we know about the reported violence between him and Brenda, but none of it was ever proven. At the writer's group, he's a good imaginative member of the clan. He writes with heart and I don't believe he is capable of murder. Anyway, why would he be at all bothered about being sacked when he's just won two million on the lottery?"

John Wilson was also sacked. I know that 15 years ago he wanted Burrows job and Terry Lennox passed him over. I've heard some rumours about things that he said in the Feathers and he was surely angry. At the writer's group, he comes across as a philosophical, God-fearing Christian, a church-goer. Again, I find it difficult to imagine him harming anyone. It would be useful to have a chat with George in the Feathers to see if he heard what John said while he was angry.

Yes! I need to have a chat with both David and John to illuminate the full picture of what has been happening. It will also be necessary to question Terry Lennox and George."

He had just about finished his first personal assessment of the crime and the vodka bottle was nearly empty. It was late, gone eleven, and he was ready for bed. Suddenly the phone rang. It was Superintendent Collingwood from Englesfield Division. At the end of the call, he slumped back in his armchair deflated and talking to himself.

"Oh joy, deep joy! Once again I get relegated to the assistant detective role. I am Mr. Nice Guy and in their infinite wisdom they've brought in Mr. Nasty Bastard from Englesfield Division to lead the investigations: the very well-known Inspector Alan Pearson, good old Fearsome Pearson, famous for his attitude towards suspects. Everybody in the police force knows that he could get a confession from a dead man if necessary. Says that Sanderford is a little hick town where nothing worthwhile ever happens. Thinks that I'm a useless detective. Shit! Shit! Shit! And more shit! That just makes my day."

Stuart picked up the vodka bottle and emptied it with a large swig.

Chapter 17
Thursday 15th November, Morning
Old Flame

David had woken up feeling like he'd been run over by a steamroller. He'd laid in the bed thinking about all that had happened in the past few days and decided it was time to consider Terry's philosophical advice.

"Yes! It's not the end of the road. I'm well-heeled now, so I'm going full out for a change of direction in my life."

Then he rolled over and went quickly back to sleep. It wasn't long before he fell into a vivid dream.

"I can see this beautiful sandy beach stretching on for miles. The soft white sand is cool underneath my feet as I walk along barefoot on the tideline, teasing my toes in the water. Warm afternoon sun caresses my skin and a refreshing light breeze makes me feel alive. An unblemished tall and cloudless butterfly blue sky soars high above my head. In the distance I can see perfect mountains laying like a dark snaking ribbon across the horizon. I am walking hand in hand with someone very special. We smile and stop to kiss in the precious wonder of a stolen moment. We are two tiny specks in the vastness of space, lost in the love that we share. We stop spellbound and kiss again.

Crash! Like a thunderbolt I fall into another dimension.

I am sitting in my armchair flicking through the pages of a book. It's an address book with red covers and yellowing pages, and I find myself frantically searching for someone, someone special. All the pages pass before my eyes, cover to cover, and then this sequence is repeated over and over and again. I can feel my heart beating faster. I am taking short and urgent breaths. I am sweating. I am anxious and on edge."

David woke up with a start, feeling breathless.

Later that morning David felt somehow compelled to look for one of his old address books and thumb through it, waiting for something to jump out of the page at him. He was on the third pass of searching when he found what he thought he had been looking for.

"It's Susan," he told himself, *"She was in the dream. We were enjoying a day out on the shore, at a beach in Cornwall. I remember it so well."*

He let the address book drop into his lap and thought carefully for a few moments. An idea invaded his brain; an idea that wouldn't go away. It kept pounding at his senses, *"Do It! Do it! Do it!"*

"Hello. Have I got the right number for Susan, Susan Dennison?"

"Yes, you have. Who is that please?"

"It's David Dimmock. Do you remember me?"

"Yes, of course. You were the most important person in my life for a few years. What do you want?"

"This morning I had a dream about us on our favourite beach and something told me to give you a call. Do you remember being there?

"Yes, David, it was a lovely day, just the two of us and the never ending skies."

"Forgive me for contacting you, Susie, but was hoping that we might meet up somewhere."

"I don't know whether that's a good idea."

"No pressure and no hidden agenda. I just wanted to see you again. It's been a few years now."

"But why did you dump me? I loved you."

"I don't know. I was confused because Brenda was so struck on me. I was too stupid to see what we meant to each other."

"Are you still with that bitch?"

"No, we are finished, lock, stock and barrel."

"What went wrong with you and Brenda? She came from a rich family. Her dad owned a national chain of restaurants; they were called "Small and Cute Cuisine", weren't they?"

"Well they went bust years ago. There was a scandal about the standard of hygiene and the employment of illegal immigrants in the kitchen."

"Oh, what a shame!" Susan smiled, and added sarcastically "Such a nice girl as well."

"You've got to be kidding. She was a bitch of the first order. A money grabbing, bad tempered and selfish cow, but she clung onto me like a limpet. She knew one certainty and that was where her bread was being buttered."

"When did you escape from her clutches?"

"It was only recently that the last straw finally broke."

"What happened?"

"I have seen it coming for a long time. Over the last three years we had rows, fights, trial separations, went to Relate. They couldn't believe it."

Susan couldn't suppress a delighted " Arhh! You poor downtrodden man."

"The girl of my dreams turned out to be the witch of my nightmares." David continued.

"And I suppose that now she's history, you'd like to get back together with me again."

"No, Susan. That's not my intention. I just wanted to see you again and try to relive something good. Have a meal, go for a walk, just be together again for a short while."

"Didn't you have some good times with Brenda?"

"Of course. When her dad was king of the restaurant , all was well with us. After the lavish pretend wedding, we went honeymooning in the Alps. It was idyllic. We set up home together and for a while we were good friends and had a wonderful life. We travelled a bit. She was interested in geology and rock climbing, and I went along with it, at least the geology, but I don't have a head for heights."

"Yes, I remember that when we tried to walk up Ben Nevis."

"Recently we went to Carlison's Rocks and I'm sure she tried to kill me. She was like a very unpredictable closet terrorist. She even turned up one day with her lesbian mate Davina, poured petrol on my car and set fire to it."

"That's unbelievable. But have you come to the crunch now?"

"Well, everything between us was just a continuous estrangement, until recently when she told me she had decided she didn't want to be Brenda anymore. She wanted to be Brian and she expected me to go along with her plans."

Susan began to laugh.

"It's not funny."

"Brenda wants to be Brian and that's not hilarious? Why couldn't you help her? Did you want to be Brian instead? Or did she expect you to become Belinda?"

"I couldn't help her and I certainly don't want to be Belinda."

"What happened then?"

"Well, because I wouldn't help her become Brian, she decided to start "divorce" proceedings on irreconcilable differences. It was going to be messy, she wanted half of everything, threatened to have Jeffery put to sleep and then tried to have me arrested on a trumped up assault charge."

"Who is Jeffery? Is it another one of your acquaintances? Does Jeffery want to change from being Jennifer?"

Susan began to laugh again.

"No, don't be silly, Susan. Jeffery is my dog. He's a little wire-haired mixture of a terrier."

For a moment, there was only silence at the end of the phone.

"OK. I don't see any harm in meeting and enjoying some time together for Auld Lang Syne. But I need to tell you something important."

"Don't tell me you're married, and your husband will want to come along to keep you safe."

"No, silly! What I have to tell you, is that I'm taking up a consultant's job in Philadelphia in two weeks' time and that's why I don't mind meeting you. There can't possibly be any future in it for either of us."

"That suits me fine. All I want to do is see you again."

Chapter 18
Friday 16th November, Afternoon
Fearsome Pearson

Alan Pearson dumped his Audi A4 in the middle of the police car park and swaggered arrogantly into Sanderford police station. He waved a crude greeting with great disdain at Desk Sergeant Donnelly and went straight to the main interview room; three chairs, one comfortable and padded, two wooden and uncomfortable and one desk with a telephone. He picked it up and demanded a cup of black coffee. He felt at home, his natural habitat. The featureless grey walls and high, top of the head level windows were just the kind of place where he functioned best. There, in the dim light, the windows were obscured by dirty blinds and an overflowing cheap glass ashtray generously provided a distinctly unhealthy odour. He lit a cigarette and slumped back in his chair, the comfy chair.

Paradoxically, he was as smartly dressed as an interviewee for a director's post at a major international organisation. An immaculate black suit, light blue shirt and red tie, with highly polished patent leather grey shoes, adorned his lean and gangly frame.

He had been given a short report prepared by Stuart McPherson, explaining all known details of the incident, the events leading up to it and the people involved. He had no respect for the Detective Sergeant who had been assigned to help him on the case and decided it was time for some contemplation.

"This is an open and shut case; it's bloody obvious who did it and I'm going to nail them. McPherson's a shit detective and he wouldn't recognise a coconut in a bag of

snooker balls. He is old school; goes in for all that motive, means and opportunity bollocks. That's why he's never got promotion. He hasn't got a nose for it like I have, an instinct, the ability to smell it. There's only one way to nail a suspect and it's my way. Sniff out the guilty one and then, and only then, try out the motive, means and opportunity, and if it doesn't stick, then bloody well make it stick. That's why my clear up rate is the best in Englesfield Division. I don't care if they call me Fearsome Pearson. I've earned that moniker with hard graft and consistent results. For me, it's a badge of honour. I'll have this case wrapped up in no time. I'm not going to stand for any nonsense from McPherson. All I'll need him for is a bit of local knowledge of people and places. He won't be allowed to do any sniffing around. That's my job and I intend to make that clear to the second-rate no-hoper. I've considered the evidence of the crime scene and got an understanding of the people in the frame. My conclusion, which I'm not going to be shifted from, is that David Dimmock, John Wilson and Tania Thompson are all prime suspects and contrived together to kill Burrows. That's it! Case solved!"

Meanwhile, David was sitting in the First Class compartment of a train heading west. He had made arrangements to have Jeffery looked after by his Auntie Rose and decided to go off to Cornwall to meet with Susan.

Chapter 19
Friday 16th November, Afternoon
Rendezvous

"What a silly question." David thought.

A little earlier that day, he remembered the excitement as he sat on a crowded train from his home in Sanderford. He was going to see Susan again, meeting her at Penzance Station. He didn't know quite what to expect. Perhaps it would be a formal business-like shake of the hand or maybe it was going to be like some romantic scene from an old monochrome film. His mind wandered a while.

"Susan was so pretty. Her perfume always reminded me of summer and I would see her smiling from a mile away."

When they met outside Penzance station, it was all smiles and laughter, warm and friendly chat and a rekindled attraction to each other.

Then they had gone straight away to see Susan's mum and dad. Susan had agreed to this meeting with her parents only the day before, so that she could meet David, albeit briefly, before she left for her job opportunity in America.

In the huge, rambling, granite constructed house on the posh outskirts of Penzance, Susan's mum, Jennifer, a petite, energetic lady in a white and blue floral dress, brought tea on an ornate Japanese tray. The three of them made polite conversation as they waited for "The Doctor" to finish his surgery.

After some time, during which the polite conversation became more awkward and staccato through Jennifer's thin smile and contrived busyness, the door crashed open and there he was. Henry, with his doctor's briefcase, files under the other arm, tweed suit, brown shoes, looking puffed and harassed.

"Hello, old boy." he condescended and without shaking hands disappeared into the kitchen, a few beads of sweat breaking out on his balding head.

Jennifer followed quickly, apologetically and then David and Susan heard them talking in not too hushed tones.

"That's just Daddy." Susan tried to reassure.

Moments later Doctor Dennison burst back into the room, offered a lukewarm, limp-wristed handshake and sneered, "So, you're Donald, are you?", as if there was some doubt as to whether the visitor knew who he was.

"No, I'm David not Donald. It's good to meet you, Doctor Dennison."

"Sorry! I'm not good with remembering names. Bit of a pain being a G.P. with thousands of patients."

David nodded politely.

"Anyway, I have to ask what you are doing here and exactly what your intentions are. You see, Susan is off to America in two weeks' time and I don't want anything to get in the way of her career."

"Yes, I understand that, Doctor."

"So, if you were hoping to pick up the relationship where you left off, then you are out of luck and I'd like you to catch the next train back to England."

David chuckled inside at the suggestion that perhaps Cornwall wasn't part of England.

"Let's say that I just need a holiday and I wanted to be with someone I knew in some of my favourite places."

The doctor scratched at his chin, slowly contemplating a reply.

"Fair enough young man, but don't do anything to jeopardise my daughter's future."

Despite the awkward history of their separation, David and Susie got on really well and decided to hire a car and take a tour of some of their favourite Cornish hotspots.

"They say it's dog's life, but I'm not really sure what that means. I like it down here in Chilverton with Auntie Rose. It's not that I don't love being with my master, David; he is very good to me and I know he loves me, but this is different. Auntie has a huge garden, with lots of soft grass to roll in and lovely trees and bushes to pee on and other places to have a good sniff. She lets me out there three or four times a day. She seems to know that at this time of year, I might get cold very quickly, even though my fur has grown nice and thick. She feeds me lovely, delicious food, which she cooks herself; none of that tinned or dried stuff that I know other dogs have to eat. I get chicken breast and slices of roast beef and my favourite, which is chipolata sausages. Once a day, we go to the beach and I get to run about with other dogs, dig in the sand and paddle in the sea. It's a bit cold, but I soon get warm again running around and playing. Then when she takes me home and I'm all dirty, she doesn't make me have a bath and smell like a human, just like David does. I can sit by the fire and warm my bones and have a good lazy snooze. It's a dog's life, but it can't be that bad. I like it here and I'd love to see my master again, but I'm not sure about going home when Auntie Rose lives in what feels like my doggy paradise."

Chapter 20
Friday 16th November, Afternoon
Battles and Triumphs

After two cigarettes and two black coffees, D.I. Fearsome was twiddling his thumbs and looking forward to a beer in the Feathers, when Stuart McPherson arrived at the police station. Desk Sergeant Mick Donnelly looked up from an immense pile of paperwork, "Afternoon Stuart! His Nibs is here in Interview Room 1, wants to see you soonest."

"Nice of you to grace me with your presence Sergeant. Lets' get down to business right away." Pearson sneered, his feet on the desk.

Stuart sat down on the hard wooden chair on the opposite side of the desk as far away as possible in such a deliberately confined space, repulsed by the stench of the overflowing ashtray.

"I can't say I'm pleased to see you assigned to this case, but Collingwood tells me we've got to work together and solve this crime."

"With respect, Sir, the feeling is mutual, but you surely know the reason why I've been assigned?"

"Let me make it clear, Stuart my old chum. I'm the Man and you're the teaboy. I do the detective stuff and you do whatever legwork I instruct you to do, no more, no less. My clear up rate makes you look like a rank amateur. Get it?"

"Crystal clear, Sir. If the lecture is over, can we get on with it then?"

The senior officer looked smug and satisfied, while his assistant was unperturbed.

"The way I see it is that Dimmock has a history of violence towards his wife, Brenda, including a recent incident, allegedly on the evening of Thursday 8th November. She reported that assault at 10 am the next day and claimed that, as a result of that incident, she has sustained a nasty deep scratch on her left cheek."

Before he continued, he paused and lit another cigarette, deliberately blowing the smoke in his assistant's direction.

Stuart was repulsed. "But she could have got that any time before she reported it to Sandersford Station, which as you say was on Friday 9th November at 10 am."

"She might have even self-inflicted it to give her husband an alibi. So he committed the murder, possibly together with Wilson and Tania Thompson."

"Very good, Sir, but she's not the wife, they're not married and it is well known in Sanderford that they fight like cat and dog. At one time in the past, she poured petrol on his car and set fire to it. Besides which, none of the alleged assaults were ever pursued. It was always her word against his. So why should she want to give David an alibi?"

"Precisely! So he hasn't got an alibi. Fait accompli!"

"If that is the case, we need to find out why she accuses him of assaulting her on the night in question."

"Bollocks! Who cares? We'll need to concentrate on nailing him, not turning her over for something so petty."

D.S. McPherson had never worked with D.I. Pearson before, but he was beginning to understand how his formidable reputation arose. That said, he was also concerned at his dismissal of any information which did not fit the D.I.'s view of what happened.

"Can I point out, Sir, if you are interested in accuracy of information, that this town is called Sanderford not Sandersford."

"You're beginning to annoy me Macca. I don't give a shit whether this town is called Sanderford, Sandersford or even fucking Arsehole City. Nothing worthwhile ever happens here. It's a little shit place, full of nobodies going about their pathetic little lives like a bunch of zombies."

The bait, however poisonous, was not risen to and the D.S. reiterated, "David's reported history of violence towards Brenda was never proven and did not lead to any convictions, including for the alleged assault on 9th November, which was reported at 10 am, and not 9 am as you say. The Desk Sergeant who has handled these accusations sees them as tit for tat domestic flare-ups at worst. Until we interview David and get some details of timings from the Crime Scene Investigation Team, we cannot be sure where he was when Burrows was murdered. Was he assaulting Brenda, was he at home alone, or was he at Bridges? After that we have to consider why should he be bothered about being sacked when he's just won two million on the lottery?"

The calmness shown in the face of his superior's unnecessary arrogance was exemplary,

"Unfortunately, Detective Superintendent Collingwood has assigned us to work together and instead of being unco-operative and hurling insults, we should concentrate on solving this case."

The D.I. screwed up his face and raised his voice with true aggressive emphasis, shouting, "That is what I will do!"

Then he kicked the waste paper basket and stormed out of the room.

There was a smile as the remaining person in the room felt that he had been the victor by points in round one.

Five minutes later, the fearsome one returned. He seemed to have calmed down enough to carry on.

"What about Wilson's outburst in the Feathers? I heard that he made threats in public, graphically describing what he'd like to do to Henry Burrows. There was no holding back; he wanted to, and I quote, "Twist his bollocks off and stuff them in his mouth.""

"Admitted, he was angry. Wouldn't anyone be after fifteen years' service and then being given the chop, especially when he wanted Burrows job in the first place and was overlooked by Terry Lennox?"

"So, he's got two reasons to be aggrieved. Not getting the job and then getting sacked. He's in the frame for certain."

"Well, Sir, whilst there's no denying those two facts, anyone who knows John is aware that he is normally a gentle, quiet man, a churchgoer and the last person in Sanderford you'd expect to commit a murder. John's outburst in the Feathers is completely out of character."

"It's John, is it? Good friends are you? I know that you and him are mates who go to the local writer's group together."

"That's obviously irrelevant."

"Is that so? What about him being missing all evening?"

"Until we have some idea of the time of the murder that is also irrelevant."

Pearson sucked at his index finger and stared at the wall for a minute or two while Stuart remained silent.

"And then there's Tania Thompson. Perhaps she is not telling the whole truth about finding Burrows dead the next day."

"Everybody knows that she is a very nice girl."

"You know so much about all these people and your judgement is coloured by personal relationships with them all, so I don't think your opinions are of any consequence. Perhaps you did it to help out all your friends?"

"I'll not respond to that insult, Sir."

A sigh and shrugged shoulders was the reaction.

"Bring them all in for interviews, Dimmock first, then Wilson, then Thompson."

"We need to talk to George at the Feathers to find out exactly what John is alleged to have said and also determine the precise time he left the pub."

"We can do that later."

"And then I think you've got it in the wrong order, it should be Tania first, because she found Burrows dead, then John, because he was sacked first, and then David, because he was sacked next."

"There you go again, Macca. To you, it's Tania, John and David. To me, it's just three suspects. I am leading this investigation, not you, so

I would appreciate it if you would just shut the fuck up with your opinions."

"And I would appreciate, Sir, if you refrained from calling me Macca. I find it intimidating. Please call me Stuart; that's my name."

"You are a snivelling little snot, Macca, and I'll call you whatever I fucking well like. Just remember you are the junior detective on this case."

Perhaps round two was a draw.

Chapter 21
Saturday 17th November, Morning
Frustration and Eviction

The two detectives drove at unnecessarily fast speed round to Newcastle Gardens, one of them gripping the steering with white knuckles, while the other was staring calmly out of the window. They knocked loud and long on the front door of number 36, but there was no reply. Undaunted, the D.I. kicked in the side gate, entered the garden and banged furiously on the patio door. Nobody came and it appeared that the flat was empty. Finding that David was not home raised the Pearson's hackles and prompted further suspicions.

Stuart McPherson was laughing inside and it showed a little too obviously.

"What are you grinning at, you baboon. There is nothing funny about our main suspect going AWOL."

"Let me advise you, Sir, I've already made some enquiries and nobody knows where your suspect is. Apparently, he left home on Thursday afternoon. If you'd bothered to ask me, I could have saved us making this visit."

"You are becoming fucking annoying again. I thought I told you that I do the detective work and you do only as you are told."

"I'm on this case with you, Sir, because I have something you don't have. Because of my local knowledge and connections it is a lot easier for me to make enquiries without putting people's back up. Blundering in with a bombastic attitude does not work. Remember softly softly catchee monkey?"

"Oh, for fuck's sake shut up. I'm going to talk to Collingwood later and get you shifted off this case."

"And in the meantime, shall we carry on with our investigations?"

Pearson's face looked as if he had just been kicked in the bollocks with steel toe capped Doc Martens. He went into a surly silence as the two men walked back to the car.

"I don't give a shit what you think. He has disappeared because he's guilty."

There was no response and they hurtled like a roller coaster, but in pregnant silence, to 101, Burnside Avenue.

"We're going to interview suspect number two. Stay out of this and just observe, Macca. This is your last chance to stay with the case."

John and Mary had just finished their lunch and were in the process of washing up when there was a ring on the doorbell.

"Detective Inspector Pearson and you know who this is. We need to ask you some questions about the night that Henry Burrows was murdered."

Mary, opened the door fully and answered, "Do come in. We've been expecting you."

Stuart sat and listened carefully, watching John's mannerisms to determine if he could see anything odd in his behaviour. Pearson stood in the corner of the kitchen, standing tall and commanding above John and Mary who were seated at the kitchen table.

"You made a very serious threat about harming Henry Burrows, while you were clearly very angry at being sacked. You were overheard in the Feathers on the afternoon of Thursday 8th November. I believe the words you used were, "I'm going to get even with that bastard, Burrows. He's got a big surprise coming to him." Is that what you said?"

"I was angry. I did get heated and make threats."

Stuart interrupted, "Did you intend to carry them out, John?"

Pearson scowled at his junior

There was no answer other than a sigh.

"You were with David Dimmock, and ....."

The D.I. Interrupted, "You said you wanted to have the pleasure of seeing your victim squirm and plead for his life, while you ripped off his bollocks off and stuffed them up his arse."

"Perhaps, I did. That doesn't mean I carried out my threats."

"And did you and Dimmock then conspire together to go back to Bridges and sort Burrows out once and for all? In short, Mr. Wilson, given your threats and the fact that both you and Dimmock had been sacked that afternoon, what happened later that day was that you planned and carried out a murder."

"No, that's not true."

"Really? And do you know that your fellow conspirator Dimmock has disappeared?" After a pause in a raised voice, "Where is he?"

"I didn't conspire with anyone, I don't know where he is and I don't care for your tone. Whilst I am willing to help as much as I can with your enquiries, I think you are being quite unreasonable with the tone of your questioning and your accusations."

Stuart looked at John as if to say, "Well done!"

John was determined to be careful when answering any further questions. His memory was hazy and had only partially come back to him in tiny slices. Whilst he vaguely remembered leaving the Feathers, heading for Willow Tree Park and then needing a pee, after that there was a giant black hole until he was back home with Mary drinking loads of coffee. The only thing more that he thought happened, but was not too sure about, was that he fell asleep on a park bench.

"We'll go back to earlier in the day now." Pearson asserted, "What time did you leave Bridges?"

"Lunchtime, about 12, midday."

"And you went to the Feathers where you met David Dimmock."

"Yes."

"Dimmock left the pub at what time?"

"Maybe 1.30."

"And what did you do?"

"I stayed and had a real tank full until about 4, when George chucked me out."

"Where did you go then?"

"I went for a walk in Willow Tree Park to try and sober up."

"And do you know what happened and what your movements were until 8 pm when you arrived home?"

"I don't know. I fell asleep."

"So, you were asleep in Willow Tree Park for four hours? You expect me to believe that? I happen to know it was absolutely pouring down with rain."

Mary interjected looking at her husband, "I was so worried about you, John, and when you got home you were very cold and soaked to the bone."

Pearson persisted, "I repeat! You want me to believe that you were asleep in Willow Tree Park for four hours?"

"Obviously not. But I don't know what happened. Ask George at the Feathers. I was plastered."

"Perhaps you strolled back to Bridges in a drunken haze with the intention of doing Burrows in."

"In that state I couldn't have wrestled with a hamster, let alone murdered anyone."

"But you can't account fully for your movements, you have no witnesses as to where you were and you were missing for four hours. Don't you agree that gives us cause for concern that you were involved in a serious crime?"

"No, I don't! You can think what you like, but if I'm not under arrest, I'd like you to leave now."

"We haven't finished."

Stuart couldn't keep silent any longer "But, I think that is enough for now." and then he looked sympathetically at Mary.

Mary was very glad that her husband didn't say anything about the dream he had endured while he was asleep on the park bench. She had listened very patiently, had made tea, offered biscuits, but she had come to a point where she needed to leap to the defence of her husband. She glared at Pearson and quietly asserted, "Don't come in here with your ridiculous theories trying to pin this awful crime on my John. He wouldn't hurt a fly."

This D. I. wasn't about to be fobbed off by a gentle middle-aged lady.

"Aren't you going be a bit cash strapped now, what with this very palatial pad and all? Must have cost you a few bob to get a place here."

Mary stood up and raised her voice, "That's none of your business and, if you must know, we won't be cash strapped as you so crudely put it. We can get by easily on my salary."

"Where do you work then?"

"I'm a solicitor's assistant at Flack, Allen and Crosby."

The only reply was a frustrated screwed up face and "I see."

An uncomfortable silence fell, with nobody saying anything for at least a minute. The ice was broken when the lady of the house threatened to get her solicitor's practice involved and then she told the senior detective, "That's it! Get out before I chuck you out."

Even though it was obvious that she was physically incapable of carrying out her threat, Stuart moved towards the door looking his senior officer straight in the eyes and conceded, "OK, we're leaving."

Stuart departed with a smile for Mary and John. Pearson crawled out reluctantly, deep in an angry pit, with a face like thunder. There was a brewing period of heavy and dangerous silence as the two detectives got into the Audi A4. Then one turned to the other and spat out a venomous argument.

"That was your last fucking trick, Macca. I'm going to have you removed from the case. You just keep getting in my way."

"I'm afraid, Sir, that we need to adopt a more softly softly approach to find out what happened. I know you like to throw your weight around, but have you heard the advice, to walk softly and carry a big stick?"

"Oh, give it a rest, will you. I don't see what fucking relevance that has to catching criminals."

Perhaps that was another point's victory, but would Stuart maintain his role in solving the murder? It looked like his senior was determined to get shot of him.

Chapter 22
Monday 19th November, Morning
Detectives in opposition

The D.I. had decided it was time for Tania to be interviewed. "Come on. We're going to talk to number one bitch. She says that she found Burrows dead on Friday morning. A little too convenient, I think. She was there the previous evening with Dimmock and Wilson and thought it would let her off the hook if she pretended to find him dead."

"I believe she has left her flat and moved in with Sharon and Brenda in Coniston Close."

"Wherever! Tell me how to get there."

When Tania appeared at the door, she looked very nervous and twitchy. She let them into her flat. almost in resignation of something that would happen sooner or later. Pearson had agreed beforehand that his assistant should lead the questioning. He was very keen to play the good cop, bad cop game. But Stuart had other ideas.

"So, let me take you back to the afternoon of Thursday 8th November. I believe that was when Henry Burrows gave you the sack, after John Wilson and David Dimmock had got their marching orders earlier during the day."

"Yes, Mr. Burrows called me into his office at about 5 and told me that I no longer had a job at Bridges."

"How did you feel about that?"

"It was a shock. Out of a job, with a mortgage to pay."

"How long had you worked for Bridges?"

"About four years."

"Did you like working for Burrows?"

"It was a job and the pay wasn't bad, but he was a complete bastard to work for."

"Understandably, you didn't like him then?"

"I needed a job. It's not absolutely necessary to like your boss."

"In common with most others, you didn't like him?"

"I hated him, but not enough to want him dead."

Pearson sensed an opportunity and butted in with more than a hint of nastiness and stared wide eyed directly at Tania's face. "I think you were involved in this murder. Answer this question. Did you kill him?"

"No."

"Where were you on that evening?"

"I was at Sharon's."

"All evening?"

"From about 7 onwards, yes."

"You're lying. I think you were involved."

"No!"

Stuart raised his hand and sought to regain control.

"Now let us move forward to the morning of Friday 9th November. Tell me exactly what you did and why."

Tania took a deep breath and composed herself, "I'd left my umbrella at work and went back to collect it. That's when I found Mr. Burrows slumped under the desk in his office. At first I thought he was asleep, but when I tried to rouse him, his body was cold."

"What did you do then?"

"I called the ambulance and the police."

"Did you touch anything while you were there?"

"Yes, when I came in, I tripped over his Waterford crystal paperweight on the floor. So I picked it up and put it on the desk."

"Why did you do that?"

"Oh, I don't know. It was just a spur of the moment thing."

Pearson banged his fist on the coffee table, "You're lying! You hit him with it. Didn't you?"

At this point, Tania became hysterical and burst into tears. Stuart was sympathetic, but Pearson decided it was just the right time to go for the jugular. "Tell the truth, you lying bitch. I'm not impressed with your answers and I know that you, David Dimmock and John Wilson all played a part in killing Burrows."

A sobbing, shaking Tania screamed, "That's not true."

Stuart decided to stop the interview there and then. Before any further aggravation, he gave Tania a tissue and said, "I'm sorry we've upset you, Tania, we'll leave it there. Thank you for your help."

He grabbed a furious Pearson by the arm and struggled to move him to the door. The D.I. was enraged, boiling over with aggression, but his junior succeeded in removing him from the flat.

When they reached the Audi, Pearson got into the driver's seat, slammed the door, nearly taking it off its hinges and began spitting fire.

"We were getting somewhere. She was definitely weakening. I had her on the verge of telling the whole truth. Once again, you have deliberately hindered these investigations."

Silence.

"You've done it again, Macca. Every time we are getting close, you drop a clanger and we lose the trail. I'm becoming more and more convinced that you might have been involved in some way."

After a calm deep breath, "I think it might be helpful, Sir, if we get back to the business of solving this crime. Your persistent sniping at the difference in our investigative approaches is becoming tiresome and distractive."

The Detective Inspector shrugged his shoulders and emitted an impatient sigh, but still shouting uttered, "Oh, very well, if we must."

He started the car and screamed off with a roar of engine and a squeal of rubber. A few hundred yards down the road, he shouted again. "I suppose at your age and so close to retirement you're not going to change. It's a pity 'cause if you followed my way, you might have something new to learn about detective work."

The Detective Sergeant smiled politely and remained silent at yet another barb aimed at his professionalism.

The silence was broken after a few minutes driving back to base with Pearson asserting that the murder was committed by a gang. Stuart agreed, but added, "Not this gang, not David, John and Tania."

"Well see about that."

By the time the car reached the Police Station, he had calmed down a little. He opened the glove compartment and took out two papers. .

He waved the papers at Stuart and said, "The CSI boys sent me these two papers that were found on Burrow's desk."

"Let me have a look at them."

The D.I. handed them over to the D.S. He had already examined them carefully and drawn his own conclusions.

Stuart scanned them quickly and then said, "So the next part of our murder riddle is to find out what is the relevance of these two documents."

"I've done that already, without your interference."

"Do you think they have any relevance to the murder?"

"Perhaps, but we need to lean on Lennox to find out."

"Do they incriminate Lennox then?"

"That's what we have to find out. The first document relates to a demolition job for the derelict factory on the Percival Estate. The contract was awarded to Bridges by Sanderford Council."

"Frank Archer is a Planning Officer at Sanderford Council. I know him from the writer's group meetings, but I don't have much else to do with him. I do know that at one time he worked for Bridges and was thought to be in the frame when Burrows got the top job there."

"What else?"

"He did military service and apparently hated it, although he made Sergeant Major. But when he writes for the group it's always about military conflict. They're usually very good poems."

"I don't give a monkeys if he writes War and Peace. Do you think he would let his previous employment at Bridges affect his decisions on awarding contracts?"

"It's possible. He's not exactly a confident and assertive character. If he was subjected to a bit of pressure, it's possible he might cave in."

"Good, that's what I want to hear. My suspicion is that Lennox offered incentives to the planning department to get the demolition job and Frank Archer as Planning Officer at Sanderford Council, may have taken a bung."

Stuart was in two minds about this assertion, but he thought it was a reasonable suspicion.

"Leave it to me to dig in the shit for this one, Macca. I don't want you fucking up the investigation again." was the D.I.'s firm instruction.

The D.S. wasn't uncomfortable with that order and he knew how difficult it could be to deal with Terry Lennox, but he reluctantly replied, "Very well, Sir."

"The other paper about the night club is interesting and at the moment I don't know what relevance it has. Any ideas from your intimate knowledge of all these pathetic people and places?"

"It seems to relate to the imminent purchase of the Neon Queens nightclub in Chilverton."

"Yes, but we are investigating a murder, so I don't see any relevance in that at the moment."

"Why would these two documents be on Burrow's desk? I heard from John, that he was fastidiously tidy and at the end of a working day everything would be filed away and the desk would be completely clear of everything, but the telephone and a paperweight."

"Leave it with me. I'm going to bust this case, Terry Lennox or no Terry Lennox, and I'm ordering you to keep your snoopy nose out of this, Pinocchio."

While these discussions were proceeding, John Wilson had been wringing his hands and praying in St Catherine's. He was troubled about his clash with Pearson the previous Saturday and he still had a vast black hole in his memory for the Friday evening. He had tried six times that morning to contact David on his mobile to see if he could throw any light on his dilemma. In the gloom of the dimly lit church, he became very agitated and had to be calmed by Mary, because he hadn't managed to receive a reply from David and had been always diverted to voicemail.

Chapter 23
Monday 19th November, Afternoon
The Lennox connection

It was a gloomy afternoon, overcast and drizzly. The sky was yellow and there was no chance of sunshine poking through the billows of dirty black clouds. At the best of time the grimy windows of interview room number 1 were reluctant to let in a small glimmer of light. Smoke filled the dank air. The stench of the butt filled ashtray was overwhelming. It was cutting at the back of the D.S's throat, as he growled a question.

"So far, Sir, we've interviewed John and Tania, but we've not seen Terry Lennox. How do you think our case is progressing?"

Three cups of strong black coffee had done nothing for the D.I.s moody attitude. The D.S. waited patiently for a spark. Pearson shot up out of the comfy chair and snarled, "Terry Lennox is Mr. Big in Sandersford."

"Lennox is as slippery as a bowl of jellied eels."

"Is he indeed? That's no bother, Macca, I'm like a Canadian Mounty. I always get my man."

"He didn't get to be Mr. Big by endearing himself to anyone. He's a major employer in this town with his portfolio of six companies, but he's no philanthropist."

"Remind me of what services his companies provide?"

"His interests cover companies in Planning, Construction, Building Supplies, Plumbing and Heating, Buildings Maintenance, and Demolition.

"He's got be pulling strings somewhere and I want to know the reasons for the sackings at Bridges. Stay here. I'm going to see this Lord of all he surveys."

"It's Monday afternoon. He'll probably be at the Sanderford Golf Club."

A little while later Pearson was meeting with Terry Lennox alone at the Sanderford Golf Club. They had a sandwich in a fairly quiet corner of the clubhouse.

"I need to speak to you, Mr. Lennox."

"I've just finished a round on the Buttermere course and played like the fairy godmother. I'm not in the best of moods. Can it wait?"

"No, I'm investigating a murder and you need to answer some questions for me."

"Very well, if you insist, but make it quick and keep it quiet. I don't want any fuss in my clubhouse."

"What time did you let Henry Burrows know that you were sacking him?"

"It was about 5.30 I got him to dismiss John Wilson, David Dimmock and Tania Thompson earlier during the day and then I phoned him to give him the push."

"Why did you do this? Bridges is a successful operation, isn't it?"

"The planning side of Bridges is no longer viable, so I've sold out to Cousins Construction. Have your heard of Cousins Construction?"

"Yes!"

"Then you'll perhaps know what a cut-throat ship they run. I could no longer compete with the way they do things, so selling out to them seemed to be the best solution."

"What about the construction side of Bridges?"

"I'm moving the construction side to Andersons, another one of my companies."

"How many companies are under your umbrella?"

"Six at present, but I am rationalising down to three."

"Why?"

"It's really none of your business, but if you must know, I'm diversifying."

"Diversifying into what?"

"The reason I'm selling off three off my operations is because I plan to take over the Neon Queens nightclub in Chilverton and possibly develop it into a casino."

"That's interesting. What other companies are you closing down to finance that?"

"Strictly speaking that is confidential, so keep it quiet, but between you and me..."

"Go on."

"I'm closing Damsonia Holdings and AGFU, but they don't know yet."

"And that will leave you with?"

"Andersons, Hammonds and one more. Look! I don't know why you are asking me these questions. Can we get it over with?"

"I've nearly finished. I needed to know the context in which you sacked Henry Burrows."

"Well, now you know."

"Just a few more questions."

"OK, but be quick, I've got work to do this afternoon."

"When you sacked Burrows, how did he take it?"

"Stupid question! Badly."

"What did he do or say?"

"He swore and cursed."

"Detail please!"

"Can't remember, but he was angry as you would expect."

"Finally, Mr. Lennox, can you tell me where you were on the evening of 8th November?"

"I was at home all evening."

"Can anybody corroborate that?"

"Yes. My wife and my son and daughter. We were all here having dinner."

"And after dinner?"

"It had been a hard day, so I fancied a game of poker. I called up my chauffeur and another card player to invite them over."

"Their names?"

"Arnie Spencer and Lenny Blunden."

"I see."

"Now, if you have quite finished, I have work to do and I'd like you to leave."

"May I remind you that this is a very serious matter. We are investigating a murder and your complete co-operation will be required. I may be back with more questions."

Without further ado, Terry got up to go to the bar to talk to another golfer. Body language implied go now, I've had enough. It was imperative for Pearson to have one last parting shot. He didn't hesitate to get back into the job.

"What about the murder?"

"What about it?"

"Do you know anything that might help?"

"Look! It's nothing to do with me. But if it helps, you could find at least twenty people who have reason to want to hurt Burrows. I can't say whether any of them are brave enough, or desperate enough, to want to murder him."

"Are you brave enough to murder him?"

Lennox suddenly began to laugh derisorily, as if he had been asked the most stupid question in history. "You're not much of a detective if you think that anybody would answer that question. Get out of here before I get the Club Secretary to throw you out."

The largely fruitless interrogation had left Pearson angry and visibly frustrated. Later that afternoon, he was banging the desk and sitting wild-eyed and red-faced when his D.S. came into the room.

"You don't look very happy, Sir, something wrong?"

A sneered reply came quickly, "You're such a perceptive bastard, know all, Macca. I don't need your sympathy and I don't want you interferring with this case again. Lay off and leave me to do the real detective work."

"There's no need to bite my head off, Sir. I only wanted to know you if you have found out anything new recently."

"No! Nothing! I went to see Terry Lennox, the devious, smart arse and got nowhere with him. But I'll go back sometime soon and do another job on him. His demeanor was not altogether helpful, but I can sniff a bit of defensive behaviour when I see it. He is hiding something, I'm sure."

"Yes, Sir, if you say so then that would seem to be very likely."

"Before I go to see him again, I want you to check the phone records. First of all, I want to know what time he phoned Burrows to sack him. Then, I want to know who else he phoned that evening on either his landline or his mobile. Exact times and duration of calls are what I need."

Chapter 24
Tuesday 20th November, Morning
Deal or No Deal?

Brenda, Sharon and Tania were having a coffee morning in Coniston Close, sitting among the grubby cushions on the ready for the dump sofa, with the cheap, scruffily hung, five-year-old beige curtains, still hiding the morning gloom. It had been raining almost continuously for five days. Parts of willow Tree Park were a foot under water. Only the ducks were happy.

"So what are you going to do now that you've left David?" asked Sharon.

"I hope I can stay here with you, my soulmate. Anyway, I'm not going back. Me and David are finished and now I need to make arrangements to become your partner and spend the rest of our lives together."

"When will you become my Brian then?"

"As soon as I can get the money together for my operations."

"David's got plenty of dosh now. Can't you screw him for big bucks? You've been living together for many years. Surely he owes you."

"He doesn't think so. Says I'll get nothing."

Tania had been listening.

"David's a good man, why don't you appeal to his better nature."

"Don't be stupid, Sis." interrupted Sharon. "He'll be cock-a-hoop about his lottery win. His good nature will have flown out the window."

Tania added, "How's about you tell him that if he gives you some sort of settlement, you'll stay off his back and won't trouble him again. That might just work."

"Now that is an excellent idea." said Brenda.

"And then you could use the money for the operation. That would make me very happy." smiled Sharon.

"We could be happy together."

"You've got his mobile number. Strike while the iron is hot, babe. Call him now. Go on!"

A windy beach in November stretched out ahead of them, as David and Susan enjoyed the cold air and wild sea at Perranporth. They were wrapped up warm and in each other's company felt warm inside. Their relationship had been rekindled. Relaxed and contented, they had walked arm in arm, smiling and hugging all along the sandy trail from one outcrop of rugged cliffs to the other and back again.

"Time for a cup of hot chocolate I think." smiled Susan, "What about that little cafe on the corner."

"Great idea, race you there, last one buys the drinks."

"No need. I'll buy them. With your long legs you'll beat me easy."

"All right, let's stroll over then."

Soon they were sitting in the warmth of the Candyfloss Cafe, sipping gratefully at their piping hot drinks.

David's mobile rang. He recognised the number. It was Brenda. He ignored the call.

Three more times it rang, same number, same response from David."

When it rang for the fourth time, Susan said, "Whoever that is, you'd better answer it or they won't go away and leave us in peace."

"It's Brenda. I don't want to speak to her."

"Tell her politely to leave you alone. Go on, David, do it for our peace of mind."

Reluctantly, the next time the mobile rang, David answered.

"David, it's me."

"What do you want?"

"I have a proposition to put to you."

"Do I need a proposition from you?"

"No, but listen."

"I don't want to."

"Please!"

David sighed, "OK, be quick."

"If I promise to leave you alone, will you give me some money to help me?"

"Why should I?"

"Because if you don't, I'll hound you until you do and you know how persistent I can be when I've got the bit between my teeth."

David looked at Susan, and turned away.

"Almost whispering, he replied, "OK, you bitch, how much?"

"A hundred thousand. That won't make much of a dent in your lottery win."

"You must be off your chump woman."

"No, I'm serious. A hundred grand or I'll pursue you like a pack of hungry wolves until you're mincemeat."

"What's it for?"

"My sex change operation. Remember Brenda becomes Brian and lives happily ever after without a tosser like you in his life."

David really enjoyed being with Susan and even though she would be off to Philadelphia in a few weeks, he had no desire to endure any trouble during the short time they would be spending together.

"Fifty grand, and that's my last offer."

After a short pause, "Its deal, but only if you send it electronically today. Every day you delay the money goes up until you cave in."

"I'll do it this afternoon."

Without a hint of thanks, Brenda put the phone down.

"Another hot chocolate, Susie?"

"Oh, that would be nice."

"I've got shot of Brenda once and for all, but it cost me a bit of money."

"That's your business, David, I don't want to talk about that gold-digger, OK?"

Back in Sanderford, Brenda and Sharon were dancing around the room, all smiles, whooping with joy.

"Got fifty grand out of the stupid wanker. This is the start of my lovely life with you, my love."

"Well done, my Brenda or should I say my darling Brian."

Nearly at the bottom of the second hot chocolate, David's mobile rang again. He wasn't too pleased with being interrupted yet again in his cosy chat with Susan.

"You're a popular man today, David. I hope that's not gold diggers anonymous calling you again for another slice of your lottery win."

"No, it's my former work colleague, John."

"Good, you'd better answer it and then, for God's sake, turn the bloody thing off, will you."

"Hello, John, what can I do for you?"

"Sorry to bother you David, but I need your help. I've been trying to get in touch with you for days."

"OK, well you've got hold of me now. What's up?"

"You know that when we met in the Feathers after Burrows sacked us…"

"Yes."

"Well, after you left you know I got completely sozzled and then George chucked me out at four, but I didn't get home 'til eight."

"Getting sozzled was very out of character for you, John."

"The police want to know what I was doing. They think I went back to Bridges with you and Tania and killed Burrows."

"Oh, John, that can't be true."

"David, there's a big gaping hole in my life for that four hours and I was wondering if you can fill in any of the blanks for me?"

David cast his mind back to that night in Willow Tree Park and remembered taking Jeffery for a walk. He recalled how the weather had suddenly changed. He shivered at the thought of the freezing rain and the massive hailstones that pursued it. Then after sheltering by the lock-keeper's house, he had made a dash for it with poor drenched Jeffery lagging behind."

"Do you remember anything about that night? All I can fathom is needing to go for a pee behind the bushes and then falling asleep on a park bench. Nothing else has come back to me."

David plumbed the depths of his memory while John waited, then a spark came to him.

"I can't say for certain, but I thought I spotted you coming out from behind the bushes in the park. The rain obscured my view through my glasses. I'm not sure if it was you or not."

"So you may have seen me? About what time was it?"

"Let me think back. Maybe 6-ish. That is when I usually take Jeffery for a walk."

"So, if George chucked me out at four and you saw me at six in the park that probably means I can account for about two hours."

"Hold on there, John. I think I may have seen you, but I couldn't swear on a stack of bibles."

"I'll just have to pray to God, that the four hour hole in my life comes back to me sooner rather than later."

"I can't help any more than that. John."

"So, you are not sure?"

John's reaction at the other end of the phone decayed into silence.

"Thanks David, sorry to bother you."

John had been almost brought to tears in the angst of not being able to remember more of what happened between getting chucked out of the Feathers and arriving home. Here he was, grasping at straws.

A short while after sealing a deal with David, Brenda went to David's empty flat, loaded up her Ford Ka with everything she needed for a few days away and disappeared.

Back at Sanderford Police Station, Pearson was casually smoking his eighth cigarette of the day and being his usual nasty self.

"Right, Macca, listen carefully. I've talked to Superintendent Collingwood yesterday evening and you can expect to be removed from this case shortly. You are massive hindrance to making progress with your wishy-washy ways."

Stuart remained expressionless and calmly replied, "I've already heard from the Superintendent and been told that there have been complaints about your behaviour and your methods. He told me that I will be kept on this case because my local knowledge is invaluable."

"Oh, for fuck's sake, Macca, you a complete pain in the arse. Your approach to detective work is positively Jurassic. And where has it got you? I am different! I don't follow procedures and I get results. My record of nicks speaks for itself."

"And he also told me to make sure that you do not bully or intimidate me."

Pearson stared daggers across the room. He didn't believe what had been said and replied with irritability, "We shall see."

Stuart stared at Pearson, thinking, "He's smartly turned out and gives an impression of complete confidence, but everything about him stinks."

Chapter 25
Tuesday 20th November, Afternoon
Crime Scene Investigation

The detectives were just about to discuss where they were with solving the crime, when Pearson got a phone call from Superintendent Collingwood telling him to rein in his aggressive attitude. He insisted that Stuart would stay on the case and that there must be co-operation or changes would be made. At the end of the call, Pearson slammed the phone down in frustration and glared daggers at his assistant.

"You've been snitching to Collingwood again."

"He rang me last night to ask how it's going and I told him where we were with the investigation. I said we had made a little progress, but were waiting for the Crime Scene Investigation report and other information from the Coroner's office."

"Why didn't he call me? I'm the leading detective on this case."

"You'll have to ask him that, Sir,"

"You really are a snotty faced little creep, Macca, and I wake up every morning regretting that I have to work with you."

"Can we get on with our investigations, Sir? Your antagonism is getting us nowhere."

"Oh, well, I suppose I'm stuck with you for the duration, but try not to get up my nose too much."

"I am sure we can work effectively together, Sir, if we leave the animosity aside. I believe that envelope on the desk is what we've been waiting for; the findings from the Crime Scene Investigation and the Coroner's report."

"Yes, so what?"

Have you had a look at them yet?"

"Got them late last night and perused them as bedtime reading."

"Shall we discuss the findings then?"

"I can do this perfectly well on my own without your interference, but if I don't share the information with you, you'll only go kowtowing to Collingwood again."

"Let us begin then, Sir."

Pearson began to read the Coroner's report. "Time of death is estimated to be between 7 pm and 8.30 pm and a post mortem determines that the cause of death was a brain hemorrhage due to a blow to the right side of the head with a heavy object."

"That's more or less what we expected. Anything else?"

"Yes, hospital records show that Burrows was taking medication for a heart condition. He had serious furring of the coronary arteries and would have been suffering bouts of angina."

"Might have explained his nasty and unpredictable behaviour? What about the Paracetamol?"

"I phoned Burrows G.P., Doctor Phillips, this morning, and he told me that Burrows was addicted to prescription drugs, especially Paracetamol."

"Had he taken any that day?"

"Yes, but examination shows that he had only ingested a small amount."

"That's interesting. We know already that a quantity of Paracetamol was spread across his desk."

"And so?"

"So that leads us to a number of unanswered questions, starting with: was there an attempt to kill him by forcing him to swallow a large quantity of Paracetamol?"

"If that is the case, then that must have failed, because he'd only ingested a small amount."

"Maybe he resisted swallowing them. He's not a puny wreck."

"I know, I played golf with him once. He's an animal. I didn't like him."

"Join the club. He didn't have any friends."

"So, if he only swallowed, say, two Paracetamol, why were the others strewn across the desk?"

"Maybe it was a bungled attempt to make it look like he committed suicide because he had been sacked."

"Perhaps! So who spilled the bottles across the desk and did they do it after killing him?"

"I think we can draw some conclusions from those findings and our questions."

"Such as?"

"Although at first sight this looks like suicide, closer examination reveals that this as a red herring, in that he had only a small amount of Paracetamol in his blood."

"And?"

"If he had swallowed any more than two of the tablets, they had not taken much effect by the time he died."

"Right! OK! The post mortem examination of Burrows shows no evidence of an attempt to force them down his throat to make it look like suicide?"

"So, if the Paracetamol are a red herring, we have a number of relevant questions. Exactly when were the tablets scattered on the desk? Who scattered the tablets? Did someone make a pathetic attempt to make it look like suicide and why?"

Stuart was pleasantly surprised at how well he and Pearson were suddenly working together. For once, he felt that they could make significant progress on the case without the persistent bickering and abuse. However, Pearson was, within his own mind, still adamant that as the lead detective, he would sift the evidence, instruct his assistant what to do or say, and gain all the credit for solving the case.

"Shall we move on to the mystery surrounding the golf bag." asked Stuart.

"CSI say that the golf bag was found on the floor. Tania has confirmed that Burrows was a keen golfer who kept his golf equipment in a cupboard at the office. She says he was very possessive and would look after his clubs as if they were made of gold."

"That sounds about par for the course. They are monogrammed clubs with his initials embossed on the back of the heads."

"I see! So that begs the question, why was the golf bag on the floor and not in the cupboard?"

"Something else is possibly relevant. The 5-wood was missing and I'd say from playing in the Sanderford Open with him that it was his favourite club."

"Perhaps the 5-wood was used as a weapon and was disposed of after the murder."

"We are possibly on the right track with that suspicion."

"So, if it was used as a weapon, who hit him with the 5-wood?"

"That's another question that we will need an answer for."

Stuart felt that there was a strange atmosphere of co-operation towards a common goal in the way that the discussion was going. He didn't expect it to last right throughout their time together, but began to wonder what the change in their interaction was due to. It was his reasonable supposition that dealing in facts, as provided by the CSI team and not the arduous process of interviewing people, helped Pearson to focus on what was important. It was pretty obvious that, as far as the people aspect of solving crimes was concerned, the two detectives had fundamentally different approaches. Stuart interviewed, while Pearson interrogated. Stuart looked for logic in the motive, means and opportunity methodology, while Pearson made up his mind based upon instinct, a hunch or just the plain enjoyment of being nasty to suspects. Stuart went about his work quietly and thoughtfully, while Pearson jumped in with both feet and sought to bust arses.

They broke off from studying the reports at this point. Stuart went out for a walk in Willow Tree Park to clear the stench of cigarettes from his lungs and to reflect in the fresh air on new information, while Pearson drank two cups of strong black coffee and added to the mountain of cigarette butts in the overflowing ashtray on the interview room desk.

Half an hour later, they came back together.

Pearson began with, "Let's move on and look at the remainder of the CSI report."

Stuart was keen to get a full picture and agreed, "What else have we got, then?"

"Well, there are a range of very severe injuries, to the head, the right hand and left knee."

"I wonder what is the significance of there being so many injuries and particularly two to the head."

"The CSI report says that the two blows to the head, one on the left side, one on the right, were probably made with different weapons."

"So, we have to ask ourselves if there was more than one assailant."

"The injury to the left side of the head along the line of the jaw bone was probably made before the other injury and was not likely to have resulted in the victim's death."

"So it appears that was possibly inflicted with a different weapon to the other head injury."

"Yes! It's been determined that the injury to right temple resulted in death due to a brain hemorrhage."

"And if the injuries were inflicted with different weapons, that would indeed suggest more than one assailant."

"I agree with you there, Macca."

"So, what about the other injuries?"

"There is a crushed and bloody right hand, which it is suggested is the result of something like a hammer blow. Perhaps a bit odd, but there is some blood under the fingernails, a DNA blood test confirms it is not Burrow's."

"That could be an indication that he may have tried to resist the attack and managed to injure the perpetrator. If it is not Burrow's blood, then whose blood is it? Finding that out should identify a suspect."

Pearson grinned, "Gotcha! We are going to get Dimmock, Wilson and Tania DNA blood tested as soon as possible. That will confirm my suspicions. Got them banged to rights at last!"

"Maybe it will confirm that they are not guilty if there is no match."

"You irritate me, Macca. This is the breakthrough I've been waiting for. Don't ignore the obvious."

"Only time will tell. Do you want me to set up the tests then?"

"Is the Pope a God bothering, Latin reading, pervert?"

"I take it that means yes?"

"Let's move on before you piss me off anymore."

"Very well, Sir."

"Next, there's the injury to the left knee resulting in a shattered kneecap, which also looks like a hammer blow."

"I think it's reasonable to assume that whoever delivered the hammer blow to the right hand also smashed the right knee cap, and that both injuries were inflicted with the same weapon."

"It grieves me to say that I can agree with you again."

"Looks like there's more."

"Yes! On top of all that, there are bruises on the rib cage and face, which are consistent with him also having been beaten up."

"He wasn't having an altogether good day, was he?"

"We've got to wonder why there are there so many different injuries."

"Given the complete range of injuries and the likelihood that they were inflicted with different weapons, it would seem possible that this was not a single assault, but a series of incidents."

"You're beginning to get up my nose, Macca. I don't like it, but I have to agree with you again."

Pearson leaned back in his chair with a smug, self-satisfied look on his face, lit another cigarette, and said, "I think that's it. There's nothing more I need to discuss with you."

Stuart disagreed, "Perhaps the CSI and Coroner's reports have given us lots of indications, but there's something that's been nagging at me for a few days."

"And what might that be?"

"It's to do with the paperweight."

"What about it?"

"It's a heavy object, so could it have struck the fatal blow?"

"I see. Let's go over what we know." Pearson agreed wearily, "I know that the paperweight is a golf trophy from the Sandersford Open which Burrows won in August this year. He was very proud to have won this valuable trophy made of Waterford crystal."

"And according to John and Tania it was always on his desk, even at the end of the working day, after he had put everything else away. So we have to ask ourselves why there are none of his fingerprints on it."

"If he was that proud of winnning it perhaps, as a matter of routine, he cleaned it at the end of every day."

"Yes. Perhaps! The only fingerprints on it are Tania's. She says she picked it up without thinking, replaced it on the desk the next morning."

"That would explain it, but maybe she is lying. Maybe she was at Bridges that evening and hit him with his favourite trophy."

"I think that's a bit of a longshot. I can't imagine Tania attacking and killing Burrows all by herself, especially as he sustained so many other injuries."

Pearson's eyes lit up, as if he had made a beautiful discovery.

"There you are," he smiled, "We are back to my original idea, that Tania went with Dimmock and Wilson to kill him."

"But if she is telling the truth about picking it up the next morning, then there is another possibility."

"And what, pray tell, oh master detective, would that be?"

"If the paperweight was the murder weapon, could it have been wiped clean by the murderer after the fatal blow was struck?"

"A stab in the dark! No! Dimmock, Wilson and Tania murdered Burrows and that's what I am going to prove."

"Maybe there was a series of incidents leading up to murder."

"Yes. He was beaten up, hit with several different weapons, suffered a range of injuries during a prolonged attack and then finally bumped off. I know who did it, and with or without your help, I will prove it."

"Bearing in mind all of that, there are a number of unanswered questions."

"Not as far as I'm concerned."

Pearson's mood had changed back to a single-minded belligerence and a belief that his version of events and perpetrators was the only line of enquiry worth pursuing.

Stuart, meanwhile, was considering other possibilities.

"Was this some kind of ritual or revenge killing?"

"Was the crime premeditated or a mistake?"

"Was it some sort of bungled attempt at perhaps a robbery that went badly wrong?"

Pearson was certain in his narrow view. Stuart was still looking at the bigger picture.

Chapter 26
Wednesday 21st November, Morning
Lennox coughs up

Detectives one and two were back at the ranch, mulling over their deliberations.

"Did you check the phone records relating to Lennox' phone calls?"

"Yes, Sir."

"And what can you tell me?"

"Lennox phoned Burrows at Bridges, presumably to sack him, at just after 5.30 pm and the duration of call was 17 minutes and 4 seconds."

"OK, what else?"

The records show that there were three more calls around about that time. One to Arnie Spencer's mobile at 6.10 pm, lasting 2 minutes 34."

"OK."

"One to Lenny Blunden's mobile at 6.14 pm, lasting 4 minutes."

"Yes."

"And finally, a call to Peter Thornton's landline at 6.24 pm, lasting 2 minutes and 10 seconds."

"I want you to go off on your own and interview Peter Thornton. He's Lennox' right hand man, so he might be able to uncover some useful information."

"Is it an official visit?"

"Yes, tell him that he is required to help us with our enquiries."

"OK, Sir, right away."

Stuart knew that Peter Thornton would probably be at work and so he went to find him at the office of Andersons.

"Hello, Stuart, what brings you here?"

"I just need to ask you a few questions about the night Burrows was murdered."

"Why? It's nothing to do with me."

"Don't worry. It's just Pearson being himself, and wanting to know what everyone in Sanderford was doing on the evening of 8th November. Sooner or later, he'll probably call in our Lady Mayoress for questioning."

"One day, they'll catch up with the over-zealous wanker. I heard a tinkle on the grapevine that he is the worst kind of bent copper."

"He sure is giving me the runaround."

Through the writer's group, the two men had some experience of each other. Stuart knew what a control freak Peter was and Peter knew what a soft touch for a detective Stuart was. Stuart was determined to do his job, but Peter was always certain to have the upper hand.

"You were at home all evening?"

"Yes! Except when I popped out to the Tesco's Extra in the High Street to buy a bottle of champagne. The 8th November is our wedding anniversary."

"There are CCTV cameras all along the High Street and in the shop. We can check that."

"Go ahead; I've got nothing to hide."

"Did you receive any phone calls that evening?"

"I had a call from Terry Lennox inviting me to a game of poker, but I had to turn him down, because like I said, it was mine and Christine's 20th wedding anniversary. Hence the bottle of champagne."

"About what time was that?"

"Can't say exactly, but probably about 6.30 pm, just after I got back from Tesco's."

"And then you were at home all evening?"

"Yes, Stuart, like I've already told you, it was our wedding anniversary. Now, I've had a hard day, can we leave it there?"

"Yes, that'll be all for now. Thank you."

Stuart returned to base and checked CCTV and phone records and found that Peter Thornton was telling the truth.

Meanwhile, Pearson went off to meet with Terry Lennox alone at Sandersford Hall, without Stuart's knowledge. He didn't want to tell Lennox he was coming. He felt it would be more useful to take him unawares. So, he just turned up at the gates of the mansion and rang the bell. When Lennox answered, he insisted on being let in. There was a great deal of reluctance, but eventually the gates glided silently open and Pearson drove at speed up to the perfect white mansion, extravagantly illuminated in the cold darkness of a November morning and skidded his Audi to a halt, kicking up the gravel drive right outside the door.

It took a while for the ring on the door bell to be answered. Deirdre was out shopping and so Terry answered the door and reluctantly invited his visitor in. With obvious irritation he uttered, "It's a bad time. I'm very busy at the moment working on the takeover of Bridges."

The hostility between the two men was obvious and was heightened when Lennox insisted that they didn't stray any further than the hallway to have their confrontation.

"Can we sit down somewhere?"

"No, do what you need to do here."

"I need you to clarify some things for me."

"Make it quick. Like I said, I'm very busy at the moment."

"Mr. Lennox, it is very important that you co-operate with me. I am investigating the serious matter of the murder of Henry Burrows."

"OK. I'll give you 5 minutes."

"You'll give all the time I need, or there will be consequences for you."

"Let's stop haggling then and get on with it. What do want to know?"

"Can we sit down somewhere?"

"No, like I said, do what you have to do here or piss off."

Pearson was not happy to be dominated, but he also wasn't about to be put off the scent and Terry Lennox was clearly adamant about the situation. They remained in the hallway.

The D.I. wanted to talk about the two documents found on Burrow's desk.

The other document related to the purchase of the Neon Queens nightclub.

"See this document? It illustrates a potentially illegal transaction between yourself and the Sanderford Council Planning Department relating to the awarding of a contract. It implied an incentive payment to Frank Archer. We've got you banged to rights for bribing a Sandersford council official over the demolition contract at the Percival Estate and we will also be arresting Frank Archer for taking a bung."

"You're a bit naive if you don't understand how organisations carry their weight in the building and construction business. Council officials have to give planning permission for all new contracts and Frank Archer's little perk is just a necessary evil. All companies offer incentives; sometimes holidays, sometimes cash, even to pay off gambling debts. That's the way it is."

Terry was confidently asserting himself, but Pearson wanted to make him wriggle just a little. He decided to apply some pressure.

"Listen, Lennox, I've got enough shit to put you and Frank Archer behind bars. Are you going to confess to giving a bribe to a council official? It could make it easier for you when it comes to court."

"I don't know how this bribery connects with Burrow's murder. Can you help me out there?"

"It's just that this is one of two interesting documents found on Burrows' desk the morning after the murder took place and I want to know why it was there."

"I sacked Burrows, but I didn't murder him. It's nothing to do with me."

"I'll tell you what I think, shall I?"

"If you must."

"Burrows had this piece of incriminating evidence on you and was about to blackmail you if you didn't reinstate him."

"Really? That's very clever of you to fabricate that as evidence."

"I think the facts speak for themselves, and then there's another document relating to the Neon Queens."

"What about the Neon Queens?"

"I suspect something shady is going on there too, but I haven't found out what yet. There is no doubt that, sooner or later, I'll nail you for that as well."

Suddenly, the knives and forks were discarded from the duel. Terry moved to a corner and sat back in the only chair in the hallway, cupped his chin in his hands and grinned. Inside his brain some wheels were turning. Pearson waited for a reaction.

"Let me put a proposal to you. Can you turn a blind eye to the business with the demolition contract, if I come up with some useful information for you?"

"What kind of information?"

"Something that might help you with your investigations."

The D.I. sensed an opportunity to open a new line of enquiry and gain some financial reward for his pains.

"The blind eye might come with a proviso. Do you understand?"

Terry had considered his options and he knew that every man had a price. Through the grapevine he suspected that Pearson was a bent copper. He deduced that he might respond to a financial incentive to ensure the case would not be pursued, if he divulged what he knew about the night Henry Burrows was murdered.

The detective considered what was important to him being able to solve the murder case and said, "You paid ten grand to Frank Archer. I think it's only fair that you reward me with the same privilege. Shall we say that the two sums cancel each other out?"

"You'll have to give me a few days."

"I want it in cash."

"Is there any other way to give a bung to a bent copper?"

Pearson ignored the wind up and sensed that he was on a winner with this situation and assumed it was a way that Lennox saw of taking the suspicions away from him.

"OK! But I want to know what you've been hiding from me and I want to know now."

Lennox relaxed in the chair while the detective stood tensely in the middle of the hallway.

"You are right. Burrows was going to blackmail me about the demolition contract."

"And Neon Queens?"

"No, that wasn't it."

"What's Neon Queens got to do with this then?

"Burrows knew that I needed the proceeds from the demolition contract to fund my takeover at Neon Queens. And he also knew that there was a subsequent construction project to build a new housing estate on that site. Frank Archer was also going to be the planning officer for that job. That was the connection between the two documents that Burrows was going to use to blackmail me."

"So, what happened?"

"I needed to stop him. So I called up Peter Thornton, Arnie Spencer and Lenny Blunden to go round to the Bridges office and find those two documents."

"So the three of them went to Bridges?"

"Peter didn't help because it was his wedding anniversary."

"Who is Arnie Spencer?"

"He's my chauffeur."

"And this Lenny Blunden? What's he got to do with this?"

"Lenny is my heavy man; he's a bouncer at the Neon Queens. Whereas I knew that Arnie could be very persuasive, I needed Lenny to go with him, because he would enjoy cutting up rough if it was necessary."

"I see. And did your two henchmen find what they were looking for?"

"Yes, but what I didn't know was that Burrows must have had copies and I suppose your boys must have found them on his desk."

"So, they were at the Bridges office sometime in the early evening?"

"Yes."

"Did they tell you what happened when they got there?"

"No, I am not interested in the detail; I just wanted them to find the documents. You'll have to ask them."

"Do you think they murdered Burrows, because if they did, you could be an accessory before the fact?"

"Again, you'll have to ask them."

Pearson was happy that he suddenly had a new lead and added, "Is there anything else you want to tell me now?"

"No, that's all you're getting from me."

Terry went to the door, opened it wide and his body language clearly implied, "Go Now, I've had enough." Pearson shuffled towards the door saying, "I'll be round to collect my reward in a few days' time."

"Yeah! Piss off now before I get fed up with talking to a piece of slimy shit like you."

The D.I. felt good. He thought he had Lennox by the balls. He had no intention of sweeping Lennox' transgressions under the carpet once he'd got his ten grand.

Lennox was grinning like a Cheshire cat. He felt even better. There was something very satisfying up his sleeve.

Chapter 27
Thursday 22nd November, Morning
Chance meeting

Stuart had just left Davidson's Newsagents in the High Street after buying his daily newspaper and was walking along in the crisp morning air, ready for another day of battling with the case and with the fearsome one. He saw Sharon on the opposite side of the street outside the Pop-Inn cafe, waved and went across.

"Hello there!"

He didn't know whether to greet her with a hello Sharon or hello Davina.

"You look at bit hassled. Anything wrong?"

"I'm looking for Brenda. We were supposed to meet here at eleven, but she's not turned up. Have you seen her?" she asked.

Stuart told her, "Well, I don't know where she is at the moment, but she if you see her tell her she needs to come to the Police Station for questioning."

"Why?"

"It's in connection with David. He's disappeared. He's under suspicion for Burrows' murder. Do you know where he is?"

"No, I haven't seen him since the writer's group meeting. But it was a bit odd that he decided to quit there and then. There was no warning. At least, I didn't see that coming."

Stuart smiled and just couldn't resist it.

"You've had plenty of experience of seeing things coming in the Blow Job Chronicles."

Sharon sighed as if she'd heard that a million times before.

"Do you think that David or Brenda had anything to do with the murder?"

A detective's sixth sense noticed some hesitation.

The thought occurred, *"Why is he asking me that question?"*

Then came the reply, "David, maybe. But not Brenda. On the evening of the murder, me, Brenda and Tania were having a girl's night in at my flat in Coniston Close. We were at home sharing several bottles of Pinot Grigio."

"All evening?"

"Yes, all evening."

"Really?"

"I must get on. She must have forgotten." said Sharon and that was the end of the conversation as she strode off in the direction of the Benefits Office.

Stuart sat down in Willow Tree Park, ploughing his way through a surfeit of non-news in the local paper when he suddenly realised how significant his surprise bump into Sharon had been. He thought, *"I smell a rat. I don't really know who is, or who isn't, telling the truth, but Brenda can't have been in two places at the same time. She says she was in Newcastle Gardens being assaulted by David. Sharon says she was in Coniston Close drinking with her and Tania. Which one is the truth?"*

Meanwhile, Sharon was in the Benefits Office feverishly trying to contact Brenda on her mobile. She tried five times but got no reply.

Chapter 28
Thursday 22nd November, Afternoon
Return from Cornwall

The two detectives were sitting in the Audi.

"What's new today, Macca, are you going to confess to being involved in this murder?"

"I'll ignore that, but what I can tell you is that I've heard that David has returned home. He's been away in Cornwall with an old girlfriend."

Without another word, Pearson started the car and raced round to Newcastle Gardens as if he was Lewis Hamilton roaring off in pole position at the Monaco Grand Prix. Stuart had not even been able to collect himself from the G-force before Pearson was banging on David's door. There were no formalities when the door opened.

"You're under arrest on suspicion of committing a murder. Get dressed and come with me."

"Am I really under arrest?" asked David.

Pearson said nothing, but Stuart reassured the young man with, "No, not unless he has cautioned you."

Stuart got a withering look from Pearson.

"So what are we doing?"

"We are taking you to the police station to help with our enquiries."

"OK, I'll just put my coat on."

Minutes later, Pearson's prime suspect was roughly manhandled from the car and frog-marched into the Police Station. The atmosphere in the interview room was belligerent. The D.I was certain he had got his man.

"You did it, didn't you?"

"Did what?"

"Murdered Henry Burrows."

"You must be demented. Why would I bother? I've just won two million on the lottery and getting sacked by Burrows was a timely bonus."

"Yes! About your big win, Dimmock. We've looked at your bank accounts and there's a transaction where you give your wife £50,000. Is that for the alibi that she gave you?"

"It's Mr. Dimmock if you don't mind, and if you must know I gave Brenda, who is not my wife, fifty grand to get her off my back. She wants a sex change operation and is going to become Brian."

Pearson almost wet himself laughing. David remained silent.

When he gathered his composure, "And where is she now?"

"I don't know and I don't care. I've got the bitch off my back."

From the beginning Stuart had found it hard to imagine it was possible for David to have murdered Henry Burrows; even more so, that he had been assisted by John and Tania. The interrogator in chief chewed the end of a pencil and tried to wipe the image of someone having a sex change op off his mind.

"Am I under arrest then?" asked David.

"No, you are helping us with our enquiries." replied Stuart.

"And you'll be here until I tell you we've finished."

"If there are no more questions, I'm going now."

"Sit down!" bellowed Pearson.

""Fuck off!" replied David, as he stood up and left.

Pearson kicked the end of the desk in a rage and Stuart was sure that steam came out of his ears. He was like a fire breathing dragon. The fellow detective sat calmly on the uncomfortable chair, closed his eyes, took deep breaths and waited.

All was silence, until he said, "Well, that didn't go too well, Sir. I think perhaps a more friendly approach might be appropriate."

"It's due to your interference again, Macca. Just because I didn't caution him, you let him slip through the net. He's fucking guilty as hell."

"But there was one thing lacking there, Sir, with your approach."

"What the fuck was that?"

"Evidence, Sir, evidence."

Not for the first time in their detective partnership, someone stormed noisily out of the room.

Chapter 29
Friday 23rd November, Morning
New information

As the detective team squeezed themselves into the stench and stain of interview room 1 at the Sanderford Police Station to assess the current situation, the weather outside was atrocious. The rain of the last few days had given way to an early morning frost, thin ice in sheltered corners of the streets and a wind chill factor that cut like a meat cleaver through soft cheese.

Stuart asked, "What can we agree on?"

Pearson made a snide remark, "Where do we differ in our consideration of the evidence, Sergeant?"

"I think the trail has dried up with pursuing David, John and Tania as the gang who committed the murder with the motive that they were all sacked by Burrows. There must be something else going on that we can't put our finger on yet. We need to try a different approach, perhaps widen the net. And if you want to maintain your clear up rate, Sir, I think that will be essential."

"OK. Where do we go back to? Who is it that's not telling the truth, the whole truth and nothing but the truth?"

"No, Sir, we do not go backward, we go forward." came the assertion from a confident D.S."

"Alright, Mr. Clever Bollocks, what do you suggest?"

"Well, in connection with suspicions about David, I spoke to Sharon yesterday and she said that Brenda was at her flat drinking all evening.

"So"

"Brenda has told us that she was at David's, being assaulted. That's a loose end that needs sorting."

"Interesting! Where is she?"

"We don't know, but her car is missing. I've put out a request nationwide to see if she turns up on an ANPR."

"You should have told me about that before now. When did you do that?"

"Earlier this morning."

Silence descended on the room as the D.I. suppressed his anger at his D.S. working on his own without asking him first. It was only a small transgression, but his face was full of thunder and he managed to restrain himself. His detective opponent rode the silence looking calm and maybe, a little smug.

A change of direction ensued with, "I'm not sure about Tania; she is in a very nervous state after finding Burrows dead at the office. I think she knows something that she is not telling us."

"I thought you said she was such a nice girl and couldn't possibly have committed the murder."

"I did, but that doesn't mean she doesn't know more than she's telling."

"What about Peter Thornton then? He's Lennox's Mr. Fixit, isn't he?"

"I went to see him at Andersons to see if he might be able to shed some light on what's going on with these documents."

"You did it again, Macca, acting without my permission. Why don't you just do as I tell you?"

The D.I. had obviously forgotten that he had instructed his assistant to talk to Peter Thornton.

"You told me to do that, Sir. With respect, you need to understand that although I may be your junior, I am in a position to gain the confidence of anyone in Sanderford much more easily than yourself. Softly, softly, catchee monkey."

"Don't give me that bollocks again. If you won't follow my instructions, then for fuck's sake tell me where you are going and what you are doing before you do it. And then report back to me immediately with what you have learned."

"Isn't that what I am doing now, Sir?" said the D.S. recognising that there was perhaps the slightest sense of a softening in the D.I's demeanor towards him. He also thought that whilst scoring points over the belligerent attitude of his senior was very satisfying, it didn't take them any nearer to solving the case.

"Do you want to know what I found out by talking to Peter Thornton?"

"OK, give me the nitty gritty."

"On the evening of 8th November, Lennox phoned him to invite him to a game of poker, but he turned it down."

"Why?"

"It was his wedding anniversary and he was at home nearly all evening."

"Nearly all evening?"

"He went out to the Tesco's Extra in the High Street to buy a bottle of champagne."

"Is there more to tell?"

"I've checked the CCTV in Tesco's and on the High Street and with the telecom people and he is telling the truth."

"Been busy, haven't you. Did I ask you to do that?"

"Yes, Sir."

Another awkward silence followed, accompanied by an obviously suppressed frustration, clearly illustrated by clenched fists and a red face. Meanwhile, a sense of satisfaction at winning a series of little skirmishes flowed over the calmer person in the room.

"And then, there is Terry Lennox. I know we've still got to question him." He's a shifty piece. I wouldn't mind betting he's involved somewhere. The documents on the desk must be a clue to his part in this crime."

"Too late, Macca, I've already done that, so don't bother with him for the time being. I've had a tip off from an extremely reliable source that two no-hopers called Arnie Spencer and Lenny Blunden might be worth talking to about the documents. Do you know them?"

"I know of them. Arnie Spencer is Lennox's chauffeur and Mr. Fetchit or Fixit and Lenny Blunden is a bouncer at the Neon Queens nightclub in Chilverton. And by the way, that's not his real name. He's got form for assault, GBH and petty thieving, and his real name is Francis Cockburn."

"We are going to interview the two of them. Together! Me and you."

Stuart asks again about Terry and the documents on Burrow's desk.

"Yeah, Macca, leave it. And that's an order. I've looked very carefully at everything and it appears that there may have been an illegal incentive offered to a Council employee in exchange for the award of a very lucrative demolition contract. But at the moment, I don't think there is enough evidence for a conviction on the grounds of fraud or bribery."

The D.S. wasn't convinced. But then whenever his superior officer stated anything with such assertiveness, he was always left wondering why.

"I have a new unexpected angle that darkens the intrigue." added Pearson, "Yesterday I had a phone call from a colleague who does a bit of fresh water fishing. He was down near Cullington where the River Sander meets the River Weaver and came up with a very interesting catch."

"I hate fishing, but don't tell me it's the one that got away that weighed fifteen pounds."

"Don't be flippant, Macca. What he discovered could be important. There's been a period of heavy rainfall since the murder and a broken 5-wood with some initials on the head was washed up at the side of the river. I think it's the missing 5-wood from Burrows golf set."

"Interesting!"

"Now, let's think ahead and suppose that the murderer decided to dispose of the murder weapon by flinging it in the river at, let's say Muddyreach Bridge, just off the town square. Perhaps, if the weather was mild, it would bury itself in the mud and never be seen again. But with the torrential rain and the river in flood in the last ten days it could have been washed up the river towards Cullington Beach."

"Perhaps, it's simpler than that. Whoever wanted to dispose of the golf club thought it would be a good idea to do it somewhere out of town and threw it in near Cullington."

"Whatever! The golf club has been examined to see if it could have belonged to the deceased. After over 10 days in the river, there obviously won't be any fingerprints."

"Couldn't there be other people around with that brand of golf clubs and Henry Burrows initials?"

"Not likely. The monogram on the clubs was actually "H z B", probably standing for Henry Zephaniah Burrows. How likely is it that any other golfer has those initials?"

"Yes, I see. I never knew that his middle name was Zephaniah."

"Burrows was a big man, maybe six foot six, and having played golf with him at the Sanderford Open this year, I know that his clubs were custom made, titanium faced and oversize, with his initials engraved on the foot in italics."

"If as you say the 5-wood fits the bill, then that would indicate a potential weapon that whoever was involved in the murder chucked in the river."

"It's beginning to worry me, Macca, about how many times I have to agree with your opinions."

Chapter 30
Saturday 24th November, Morning
Confrontation

Stuart had requested assistance from the local force to find Brenda's car. After a very short time, ANPR picked the car up on Chilverton seafront and a CCTV camera revealed that she was last seen going into the Orion Bed and Breakfast Hotel two days before.

She was located there and requested to report to the Chilverton Police Station to answer questions relating to her common law husband, David's involvement in the murder of Henry Burrows.

The old Chilverton Nick, which had been purpose built in the fifties close to the seafront, had been closed down as a cost cutting exercise a few years before and was now an estate agents office. The inadequate new one was a small community house in a residential area of town, with very limited facilities and only two officers. The head man, Desk Sergeant, Charlie Ferguson, was familiar with the two detectives from Sanderford who arrived to investigate the murder case, having worked with both of them before. He and Pearson had enjoyed many a disagreement. They were chalk and cheese, whereas Stuart and Charlie were old drinking buddies. Once Brenda had been found, the two detectives from Sanderford drove swiftly down to Chilverton to interview her.

Stuart was greeted with a "Hallo, mate, long time no see. How's it going?"

The reply with a smile was, "Charlie, you old crony, still arresting seagulls for stealing chips, are you?"

The senior detective was almost ignored and this difference in the friendliness towards the D.S. and the disrespect the D.I. was afforded, annoyed him. His reaction was predictable. He blundered his way around insisting on instant co-operation and putting everyone's back up. There was a tiny room, faced with a large window at the back of the desk, which Charlie eventually condescended to allow Pearson to use.

The D.I. told Stuart to wait outside while he interviewed Brenda.

"Cup of tea, then old mate?" asked Charlie.

"Yes please, and where do you hide the biscuits?"

By this stage of the enquiries, detective numero uno had become fixated with the idea that David had bribed Brenda to give him an alibi. Brenda was sitting in the cramped room, drinking a cup of black coffee, when he barged in noisily and without sitting down, launched straight in with, "We've looked at your bank accounts and there's a transaction where you received £50,000. Is that for the alibi that you gave your husband?"

Brenda laughed at him, saying, "I haven't got a husband."

He repeated the question with more antagonism and Brenda's response was to remain silent for a long time, before she revealed that the money was for her sex change operation.

The interviewer broke out into wicked, mocking laughter.

"That's just the sort of reaction I would expect from a misogynist bastard like you; someone with his brains in his bollocks." she reacted.

It was early in the interview, but that didn't deter the D.I. from going mental, banging the desk and threatening to have Brenda sectioned for wanting to become Brian. Then he snatched the coffee cup from her hand and hurled it at the wall. He splashed his pristine blue suit in the process, which brought a wry smile to his victim's lips. Almost climbing on the desk spitting fire with anger, he raged, "Answer my fucking question you bitch, or I'll have you sent to a loony bin."

"I have answered your question, lame brain. I've told you the truth about what the fifty grand is for."

The atmosphere of antagonism in the room was so strong, it could've been cut with a blunt knife. Charlie and Stuart drank tea and listened to the uproar with disgust. Then, Pearson played what he thought was a clever game, calming quickly, sitting down and offering Brenda a cigarette, while lighting one himself. It didn't work very well.

"You can't smoke in here. It's against the law."

"Fuck off! I'm the law in here and you'd better clean up your act, or else."

"Or else, what?"

"Or else you'll find yourself going down for refusing to co-operate and for obstructing a Police Officer in the execution of his duty. Women's prisons are not nunneries you know. They eat each other for breakfast in there and you, little Miss Cantankerous Catflap, wouldn't last five minutes in there, before they gobbled you up and spat you out in bubbles."

Brenda, or was it her Brian persona, just sat there and smiled, as her nemesis became ever more irritated.

"Can you tell me why you disappeared from your flat in Sanderford so soon after the murder of Henry Burrows?"

"I had a flaming row with David and had nowhere to go, so I thought I might buy a kiss-me-quick hat and eat some candy floss at the seaside."

"In November?"

"Alright smart arse; it was a woolly Christmas jumper and a bag of chips. So what!"

There was a pause in the interrogation just at the moment that Pearson noticed the coffee splashes on his suit. The interrogator was seething with anger. He stood up again and shouted, "Where were you exactly on the night that Henry Burrows was murdered?"

"Let me think about it. Was I wind-surfing in Tenerife or Bungee-jumping in New Zealand? I know, it's all come flooding back to me now. On the night in question, I was at my home being assaulted by the man you think is my husband."

"I don't believe you."

"Tough shit! How do think I got this fucking gouge on my cheek? Did I do it to myself with a bread knife?"

"That is entirely possible." Pearson stated and sucked in a hard breath. "Can you tell me, if David Dimmock assaulted you on Thursday evening, why did you not report it the police until 9 am on Friday morning?"

"That's 10 am not 9. I was shaken and upset and didn't know what to do."

The D.I. couldn't imagine that Brenda would be shaken and upset by anything. She didn't appear to have a softness or fragility in her behaviour. He thought that she would be aggressive and antagonistic if struck by lightning, let alone by a cut on her cheek and would want to instantly report an assault."

"I don't believe you. You are a lying bitch."

Brenda felt that there was no need for a reply.

"We've examined the contents of your car's boot."

"And?"

"And we've found something interesting."

"A herd of wild elephants?"

"No! We found a hammer in the boot."

"Maxwell's silver hammer, was it?"

"Very funny! No, it was what is known as a rock hammer."

"It's a fair cop. You've rumbled me Mr. Eversoclever. I'm interested in geology and that's just a tool of the trade. It's not illegal is it?"

"Use of it as a murder weapon is."

"OK, so go and arrest every geology enthusiast in the country for that stinking rancid pervert's murder."

"I see, you didn't like our Mr. Burrows."

Brenda turned to face her interrogator directly, implying that she had something very important to say. "When she was eight years old, your Mr. Burrows forced my sister, Sharon, to give him a blowjob. For the next four years, he persisted in sexually abusing her, until she was eleven, when he raped her. Perhaps you think he deserves a medal? I think he deserves to have his bollocks ripped off and stuffed up his arse."

Pearson thought, *"Have I heard that before somewhere?"*

"So it is your rock hammer?"

"Excellent detective work, you should get a medal for deducing that."

Brenda had never shied away from any confrontation and she wasn't about to do it now with what she considered to be a jumped up nobody with a bad attitude. Pearson cringed inside at getting nowhere, but perhaps secretly recognised with grudging respect that, in terms of nastiness, he had met his match. He terminated the interview in a demented rage, having got nowhere with his questions. Frustrated he bellowed, "Get out of here you fucking bitch and make sure that when I come for you again, you're ready to be knocked out in round two."

Brenda got up, smiled, and replied, "A useless wanker like you wouldn't last two rounds with me. Go fuck yourself!"

The bit between his teeth left the D.I. foaming at the mouth, and his perfect solution, attributing the crime to David, together with John and Tania was failing to make any progress. He was still convinced that David had given Brenda £50,000 for an alibi, but he was having difficulty proving it.

He called Stuart into the interview room still chaffing at the bit.

"Sounded like your interview didn't go to well, SIr. Perhaps you need to brush up on your technique a little?"

"Have some respect for a superior officer, Macca. I do things my way and they always work in the end," came a red-faced retort.

"I don't think threats and intimidation get you anywhere."

"Oh, really! And that's why my clear up rate is top dollar and yours is non-existent."

"That's as may be, but here in Sanderford, a softly softly approach to dealing with people is much more likely to pay dividends. That's why I have been assigned to this case and why Superintendent Collingwood wants me to stay on it."

"Oh, for fuck's sake, why can't he see sense? Collingwood's a brainless non-entity; a new breed copper more interested in justice than nicking criminals."

There was a short period of agitated silence while some wheels were grinding and then Pearson had what he thought was a light bulb moment. He took a deep breath and for the first time in recent days, he smiled at his fellow detective.

"Right! What I want you to do is question David Dimmock again. Only make it a casual, friendly, matey conversation. That's what you keep telling me you are good at. Try to appear to meet him by accident. I tell you what. Catch up with him in the Feathers. He likes a drink in there, doesn't he?"

"Yes, Sir, I can do that. What do you want me to clarify then?"

"I want to know more about how he came to give Brenda the fifty grand. We've got to persuade him into admitting it was to give him an alibi at the time of the murder. He had the motive, the means and the opportunity. That's what you, Mr. Expert Detective, use as your number one criteria in the rulebook, isn't it?"

"OK, Sir, I'll do that as soon as it becomes possible. Perhaps he'll be in the Feathers this lunchtime."

"Oh, and Macca, one more thing. You report back to me, word for word immediately. I'm going to nail Mr. Millionaire Dimmock."

Chapter 31
Saturday 24th November, Lunchtime
Changes of Direction

Fortune was on his side, because sure enough Stuart caught up with David in the Feathers that very lunchtime and managed to strike up a friendly conversation without much effort.

"Hello, Stuart, fancy a pint? I'll get them in."

"Yes, that'll do nicely."

The two writer's group colleagues sat down by the welcome comfort of a roaring log fire.

"You look a bit hassled, Stuart. Is everything all right?"

"Oh, it's just Pearson. He's a real pain in the arse to work with."

"Are you getting anywhere with solving the murder then?"

"Slow but sure, David, slow but sure."

Both men took a sup and then continued.

"The grapevine said that you interviewed Brenda."

"I didn't, but the top dog did. I heard them shouting at each other in the interview room. I think he lost the battle."

"She's an awkward, vicious bitch. But I don't know why she was questioned. Does Pearson think she's involved in the murder?"

"No. That's very unlikely, but he wanted to find out why she disappeared just afterwards and how come you paid her fifty grand."

"I don't know why she disappeared other than that's what she usually does after we've had a row."

"I know she's reported you for assault a number of times, but as far as I'm concerned, she's telling porkies."

"Yeah, and she did it again after that night. She's like an active volcano. Her nastiness is never far from simmering to the surface."

"She's got a nasty gouge out her left cheek. Says you did it."

"Never touched her. She's lying again."

"I understand that it's a fiery relationship and she said you had another fight with her the evening after you were sacked at Burrows. Did you?"

"Well, we had a furious argument, but just like all the other times, she decided to tell your lot I had assaulted her. It wasn't true. She got very angry that I didn't tell her immediately that I had won the lottery and then she dropped a bombshell saying that she wanted a sex change operation to become Brian. When I laughed, she went off in a huff and then came back several times while I was trying to watch the Merseyside derby on the box. She got more and more heated, threatening to skin me for my lottery win, have Jeffery put to sleep and then she stormed out saying she was going to Sharon's."

"What did you do?"

"Carried on watching until the match finished. It was a great game and Liverpool won 4-2."

Stuart smiled. Keeping the conversation natural and friendly he asked, "Who scored the goals?"

"Saleh got two, Firmino got one and then there was a stonewall penalty late on in the game, which VAR wiped off before a bizarre goal in injury time."

"Bizarre? What happened?"

Liverpool were on the attack and the ball was kicked away from the penalty area to very near the half way line. Henderson came racing in and fired a pile driver back towards the goal. Unfortunately, it sliced wildly to the left. The referee was just putting his whistle to his mouth to blow for full time when the ball stuck him full in the face and knocked him out cold. The ball looped up in the air, way above everyone in the penalty area and then fell behind the Everton keeper into the net. VAR decided it was a goal because the referee had not actually blown his whistle, but the match ended because the signal for full time was in progress."

"What about the ref?"

"Took them 5 minutes to bring him round and he lost two front teeth in the incident."

"What happened then?"

"Well, the match was over, but when Jurgen Klopp was interviewed he said, tongue in cheek, that the ref should have got a red card for dangerous play."

"You watched it all then? Sounds like a very good game."

"Nearly all. Brenda pulled the plug when she came home spitting fire and Liverpool were already 2 nil up after 10 minutes. I missed a minute or two and then later on, I had a phone call from my Dad, just after half time. He droned on a bit, but I kept one eye on the game."

Stuart downed his pint and went to the bar to get two refills.

"She wants the fifty grand to pay for the sex change op, then?"

"Yes, and I reluctantly agreed to give her the money to get her off my back."

"Pearson is fixated that you gave it to her so that she would give you an alibi at the time of the murder."

"That's rubbish! I wouldn't have murdered Henry Burrows for sacking me. In a way he did me a favour at a very beneficial time. He was never nice to anyone, but he had his own problems to deal with and I felt sorry for the stupid old git. It's not so easy for John and Tania, they haven't become rich overnight like me, but there is no way that either of them are involved in the murder. Besides which you must agree that I have a perfectly good alibi, as I have just explained."

Stuart was satisfied that he had resolved the matter and so the conversation moved away to another area.

"What about the writer's group? Are you coming back? We need you there for balance."

"Well. I've thought about it and decided that for the time being I'll return. I don't know quite what the future will bring me now. I'll be there on Wednesday."

By the time they left the pub, Stuart felt that in the cause of making progress with solving the case, the investigation had come to a point where Pearson's initial murder suspects, Tania, David and John, needed to be completely eliminated from suspicion. He knew that Pearson was desperate to solve the crime. So far the investigation had clearly dried up on him. He felt that a change of direction and approach would reap more dividends.

While Stuart had been talking to David in the Feathers, Pearson decided that he would use the opportunity to corner two suspects. Following the information he'd got from Terry Lennox, he had his D.S. out of the way and it was prime time for him to talk to Arnie Spencer and Lenny Blunden without what he saw as hindrance.

He found Arnie outside his flat in Coniston Close, washing and polishing Terry Lennox' Rolls Royce.

"Are you Arnie Spencer?"

"Who wants to know?"

"I'm Detective Inspector Pearson. I'm leading the case investigating the recent murder of Henry Burrows."

"So what?"

"I've been talking to your boss, Terry Lennox, and he has told me that on the evening of 8th November, he instructed you to go with Lenny Blunden to the Bridges office in Taplow Street and retrieve some papers regarding a demolition contract on the derelict Percival Estate and the purchase of the Neon Queens nightclub."

"My, my, you have done your homework, haven't you?"

"Is it true? Were you there with Blunden?"

What Pearson didn't know, was that Lennox had spoken to his chauffeur and persuaded him to admit being a party to the incident involving Burrows getting beaten up. Bearing in mind that this was a murder investigation, Lennox thought it was the best way to take suspicions away from Arnie and Lenny.

"Yes, it's true."

"OK. What time did you get to Bridges and what happened there?"

"Lennox called up Lenny and me to go to the office and find the paperwork you mentioned. We got there at about 6.30 pm.

"Burrows didn't want to co-operate. He got nasty and took a golf club out of his golf bag, swinging it around and threatening us."

"Was it a 5-wood?"

"I don't know, I don't play golf, it's a bloody stupid game."

"What happened then?"

"Lenny got hold of Burrows and wrestled the golf club from him. During the struggle, the 5-wood, if you say that's what it was, ended up on the floor."

"And then?"

"Lenny came on really heavy and told Burrows he wanted the documents or else he would kill him. I saw Burrows' briefcase under the desk, picked it up and emptied it out. The two documents fell out, together with several bottles of Paracetamol. I took the documents off the desk and then looked at the set of golf clubs. I was incensed. I can't play for toffee and I hate golf and golfers. I said to Burrows, "You tried to hit me with that club, you bastard.", and I was going to hit him with it while Lenny was holding his arms behind his back."

"Did you hit him?"

"No, Lenny stopped me. He just waded in and beat the living shit out of him. He just couldn't resist the idea of beating up Burrows. There was a furious fight, but Lenny was too strong. Burrows went limp and appeared to lose consciousness and Lenny thought he had killed him."

"Did he kill him?"

"I don't think so. He was still breathing when we left, albeit rather heavily."

"What time did you leave?"

"It was about 7."

"OK, we will speak to you again soon about this, but I'd get yourself a solicitor. At the very least you have involvement in GBH and at worst, murder."

Pearson was satisfied for the moment with what he had discovered, but before he left, he asked, "You mentioned some bottles of Paracetamol, what happened to them?"

"During the fight, lots of bottles of Paracetamol were scattered across the desk and floor."

"That explains a lot. Right! Now! Tell me where I can find Lenny Blunden."

"At this time of day, he could be in the Ship's Anchor in Chilverton. Likes a drink, does Lenny. He's probably an alcoholic."

The D.I. climbed into his car and drove quickly to Chilverton. He parked on a double yellow line outside the Ship's Anchor and entered the pub. There was an unsophisticated bunch of lowlifes thronging the bar. He walked straight up to a brassy looking barmaid and said, "Is Lenny Blunden here this afternoon?"

She pointed to someone playing darts.

"That's him! The fat, bald-headed wanker, in the sleeveless jacket with obscene tattoos up both arms, playing with the long-haired pervert in a dirty old parka."

"I'm Detective Inspector Pearson and I need to ask you a few questions."

"Fuck off! I don't talk to scum like you. It's against my religion."

"I'm investigating a murder and unless you want to be arrested here and now, you'll have to change your religion."

"Like I said, fuck off!"

"Last chance," Pearson smiled, "Lenny Blunden's not your real name is it? You are Francis Cockburn and you have form for GBH and petty thieving. It would be better for you all round, if you helped me with my enquiries."

Lenny might have had hands like bunches of bananas, but he was pretty good at playing darts.

"I need double top to win this game and then you've got two minutes."

The bouncer took a huge swig from his pint of lager, strolled up to the oche and fired a dart to win the game.

He turned to the pervert in the parka. "You owe me a pint, Brendan. Carlsberg Special Brew." he grinned.

"Are you ready to answer my questions, now?" asked Pearson.

"Yeah, go on then. Make it quick."

"Terry Lennox says that you were at Bridges on 8th November in the evening with Arnie Spencer, to get some paperwork from Henry Burrows. I've just talked to Arnie and he told me that you and Burrows had a fight and you beat him up."

"Yes, enjoyed it. For once, he was somebody who put up a fight, not like all these lager louts I have to deal with every night."

"You're a bouncer at Neon Queens?"

"So what?"

"Like a bit of aggro then, do you?"

"It's an occupational hazard. You've got to enjoy your job."

Lenny downed his vodka chaser and coughed.

"So, you admit to being at Bridges and beating up Henry Burrows?" asked Person.

"You're very bright for a copper, aren't you?"

"Is that a yes?"

"Yes."

"What time did you get there?"

"Don't remember."

"What time did you leave?"

"Just before 7."

"How come you can remember that so precisely?"

"I had an important evening planned."

"Doing what?"

"None of your f'ing business."

"OK, I'll tell you the same as I told Arnie. We will speak to you again. Get yourself a solicitor. I'm going to do you for GBH if you're lucky and murder if you're not."

Lenny laughed and downed his lager in one, "You're two minutes are up copper. Fuck off! It's beginning to smell in here."

Pearson was leaving the pub as he thought to himself, *"Jesus Christ, what an absolute meathead. The way he acts he'd be a perfect match with that complete bitch Brenda. Trouble is, they'd be trying to kill each other every day."*

Chapter 32
Wednesday 28th November, Afternoon
Twisting the facts

When Stuart said goodbye to David in the pub, he went back to the police station with the intention of reporting back to Pearson immediately, just as had been requested.

"It was a real stroke of luck, Sir, but I bumped into David Dimmock this lunchtime in the Feathers, as you suggested."

"I hope you gave him a grilling about the fifty grand."

"No, Sir, I kept it pally and found out quite a lot."

"Spill the beans then."

"David confirmed what Brenda had told you about the fifty grand. She wanted it for her sex change operation and he was persuaded to give her it to keep her off his back."

That knowledge didn't provoke any pleasure. This was not the information that was wanted to close in on a prime suspect.

"You've failed in your mission then. I told you to get him to open up and tell you it was so that he had an alibi for the murder. So much for the softly, softly approach."

"Not at all, Sir, I have established that they are both saying the same thing and I believe it to be true."

"You'd believe eggs were bananas if one of your mates had said it."

The D.S. pulled a face. The pain of dealing with this single-minded tyrant was beginning to drain his patience. The discussion paused for a moment and then the D.I.'s expression changed. He smiled, "Hang on though, that means Dimmock doesn't have an alibi."

"I think you may find you're wrong there, Sir."

"What do you mean?"

"Well, we continued the conversation with a talk about the night in question and whether Brenda was assaulted or not."

"She's got a nasty scratch on her left cheek. Isn't that evidence enough for you?"

"It could be in the right circumstances, but David says he didn't touch her and that the assault was a figment of her vivid imagination. He admits they had a furious argument and he described her as a vicious, nasty bitch."

"I'll vouch for that. She's Hitler with an attitude."

"Then perhaps the injury to her cheek was inflicted elsewhere."

"Perhaps, but Mr. Lottery Millionaire still doesn't have an alibi."

"I questioned him further and he says he was indoors all evening watching a game of football on the telly. It was the Merseyside derby between Liverpool and Everton, a good match by all accounts. He was able to describe the match to me in detail and he also told me there were two interruptions. The first was when Liverpool were two nil up and Brenda pulled the plug in anger. Then his viewing had been interrupted again by a telephone call on his landline from his father at about 8.15 pm."

"He could have watched the game on a plus one channel or on YouTube."

"I checked with the telephone company and they confirm that a call was made from the father's number to David's landline lasting 8 minutes and 27 seconds at 8.12 pm."

Perhaps it was game, set and match to Stuart at that point, but he could see from Pearson's face that he did not want to be convinced. Suddenly he looked ill at ease. He frowned and ran his hand across his brow.

"And so, Sir, I believe that establishes beyond reasonable doubt that your prime suspect was where he said he was, at home at the time of the murder."

A standard method for solving crimes, by selecting the culprit and then assembling evidence to prove the case, had hit the bumpers, but there was persistence, "Dimmock hasn't got an alibi."

"I believe he has, Sir."

"Believe what you want. I am not convinced."

"You've missed the point, Sir. Don't you see that what he told me means that Brenda is not telling the whole truth."

"What do you mean?"

"Brenda was apparently in two places at the same time. She says she was in Newcastle Gardens being assaulted by David, but Sharon says she was in Coniston Close drinking with her and Tania. I would ask myself which one is the truth?"

"OK, what about it?"

"David has confirmed that Brenda wasn't at Newcastle Gardens as she claimed and I've checked on that and established that he was there. So we come back to Sharon saying that Brenda was at Coniston Close with Tania and the three of them were emptying bottles of wine together."

"Like I said: what about it?"

"Isn't it obvious that someone is lying about their whereabouts?"

"Yes and I know it's got to be Dimmock. I don't care what he said to you about watching football on the box. He thinks that, just because he's won the lottery, he can get away with murder."

"Well, I believe what he said."

"You would, but you haven't got the real gumshoe's nose for this work. I will get him with or without your help."

"OK, let's suppose that he is lying. He popped out and committed the murder, either alone or with your other two prime suspects, John and Tania, and then went home and assaulted Brenda just for good measure. Then he watched the match on YouTube and when I spoke to him, he lied and said he had been at home all evening."

"Sounds like that's what happened."

"Can't be, because the timings don't fit."

"Explain!"

"OK! Lennox sacked Burrows at 5.30. Right! But he must have remained at Bridges for some reason."

Both detectives knew the reason why Burrows stayed on was because he was looking for documents to incriminate Lennox, but after his recent brush with Mr Big, Pearson didn't want to dwell too much on that. Also, the detective team hadn't been together for the interview with Arnie Spencer and Lenny Blunden to ascertain useful information about timings.

"I went to talk to Arnie Spencer and Lenny Blunden while you were otherwise engaged, and they have admitted to assaulting Burrows during an argument about the documents they were told to retrieve by Terry Lennox. They've also admitted to being at Bridges between 6.30 and 7 o'clock and Lenny had been proud to say that he had beaten up Burrows before they left with the documents."

Stuart continued, "If Arnie and Lenny were at Bridges between those two times and no-one else was present, then David and Brenda must both have been in the flat in Newcastle Gardens. Do Arnie and Lenny say that there was no-one else at Bridges while they were there?"

"Yes!"

"Then that's sorted that out."

"Very convenient. So you trust the words of a chauffeur and a bouncer."

"Bear with me, Sir. The time of Burrow's death is estimated to be between 7 pm and 8.30 pm. That's an hour and a half to two hours later and probably after Arnie and Lenny left Bridges."

"Yep! That fits with what they have told me."

"Brenda says, and David confirms, that she got home about 6.30, when he says he was watching the match. He tells us that there were two interruptions. One shortly after Liverpool were 2 nil up and another when his father phoned at about 8.15. When I checked the game, Liverpool were 2 nil up after 6 minutes. The match started at

6.45. And when I contacted the telephone company, they confirmed that a call was made from David's dad's number to David's landline lasting 8 minutes and 27 seconds at 8.12 pm."

"I don't know where you're going with this. There's nothing yet to convince me that Dimmock is not in the frame."

"Hold on!" Stuart requested, "Brenda says, and David confirms, that she left the flat in Newcastle Gardens at 7 o'clock. So, if that is the case, the alleged assault on Brenda happened between 6.45 and 7 o'clock and David said that she interrupted the match between those two times."

"Bingo! Got him! So he did assault her."

"If so, why didn't she report it 'til the next morning?"

"I don't know. We'll have to ask her."

"Anyway, back to what happened. The match started at 6.45 and finished just after 8.30, and as far as I'm concerned, I am certain that your suspect watched it all, bar the two the interruptions. He also knew about the incident at the end of the match where the referee apparently scored for Liverpool."

"And?"

"Therefore he was still at home at 8.30 and the C.S.I. boys say that Burrows was murdered between 7 pm and 8.30.

"Still don't get it."

"Don't you see, Sir, that he was at home for the duration of the match, which covers the same time slot as when we are advised Burrows was murdered: the start of the match at 6.45 'til the end of the match at 8.30."

"Hmm! What about the fifty grand then? I'm convinced Dimmock gave that to buy an alibi."

"Both Brenda and David confirmed it's for the sex change operation."

The D.I. looked deflated. His assertion concerning his favourite culprit for the murder was crumbling. It was about to crumble even more.

"Let's go back to say against all evidence, that David was involved. Then, let's suppose that he was helped to murder Burrows by John."

"OK!"

"George at the Feathers confirmed that John was absolutely plastered; shitfaced as you would say. So what possible use would a mild-mannered, God fearing man like John serve in attempting a murder?"

"Grasping at straws, Macca, I've had previous experiences with God botherers committing serious crimes."

"That's as may be. But you have to concede that in this case , it's highly unlikely, even though your church-going suspect can't account for his whereabouts."

"Alright! What about Tania?"

"Why would Tania even contemplate going together with David and John with the intention of murdering Burrows? What part could she possibly play?"

The deflation was all but complete. At last, it seemed that the superior officer might just be persuaded to abandon his obsessive line of inquiry. For once, there was no exhibition of the usual angry response to being corrected in his previously held suppositions. For several minutes there was a contemplative silence between the two men.

"There's something else you need to know, Sir."

"What's that?"

"David Dimmock submitted himself voluntarily, at my request for a DNA blood test. I told him it might help to prove that he didn't scratch Brenda, although that's not true, of course."

"So, why did you do that?"

"If you remember, Sir, you instructed me to get David, John and Tania DNA blood tested ASAP."

"OK, set that up, have you?"

"Yes, Sir."

"Is that it?"

"No, the forensics have reported that the blood underneath Burrow's fingernails doesn't match David's. So now we know that Burrows couldn't have scratched him."

"For fucks sake, Macca, that is totally irrelevant."

"Possibly, Sir, possibly."

Wheels turned in a brooding silence for a short while.

Then the D.I. piped up with, "OK, Clever Bollocks, where do we go from here?"

"Clearly somebody isn't telling the truth. We know what Arnie and Lenny did that night. They've confessed to GBH or serious assault. I think we have to lean on the never known to be co-operative, nasty little bitch, called Brenda."

"Yes, of course, she was allegedly in two places at the same time."

"And then there's the question of how did she really get that nasty scratch on her cheek?"

Chapter 33
Wednesday 28th November, Evening
Reflections

It had been nearly three weeks since David had won the lottery and it was certain that by now, every Tom, Dick and Harry in Sanderford, knew about it. It was also nearly three weeks since Henry Burrows had been murdered. Now a motley crew arrived at the Library in the Oscar Wilde Hall on the Town Square for the writer's group meeting. The gang were all there with those same two subjects on their minds. David had been to Cornwall for a few days, been interviewed regarding the murder and thanks to Stuart's diligence been all but cleared of involvement. But they all still wanted to know what he intended to do following the lottery win, being sacked by Bridges and having Brenda walk out on him. On top of that they all wanted to know what the score was with Stuart's investigations. In the intervening three weeks, the most outrageous misdemeanors committed in Sanderford were still more likely to be, either being back late with your library books or parking on a double yellow line.

Stuart was keen to get the meeting under way. Aware that all of the writer's group members may have at some time been suspected of involvement in the murder investigations, his detective's talent for spotting a change in behaviour or temperament was honed to a fine edge.

Once again, Peter Thornton bent to his need to be in charge and decided it would be best to curtail all discussion, until a convenient time during the meeting arose.

"Henry Burrow's murder is off the agenda and there will be no discussion regarding David's lottery win." he asserted. Then he added something that he was very fond of saying at every meeting, "This is a writing group not the social services."

The meeting began as usual with Peter's reading, preceded by his usual preamble.

"Sometimes heartless horses are undulating,
up and down on my not-so-merry-go-round,
like a relentless long day full of mocking hours,
and moving along never seeming to use up any of my time.
Sometimes rollercoaster thrills and spills exhilarate but terrify,
Intimidating in days flashing by, in mighty nanosecond bites,
and hurtling along, always screaming,
to abuse the passage of my time."

After that Peter looked up and said, "I've been thinking a lot about the passage of time. None of us are getting any younger and life is a battle of constant change. I have written a poem called, "Tick tock", to reflect how I feel at the moment.

"Tick went the slow, slow, slip of the sound,
Till the tock at the end of the tick came around,
And the slot in between, when the spring unwound,
Clocked an endless slice of a life unbound.
Tick tock two!
With a tick and a tock, and a fairground bound,
Rock and Roll, Up and Down, on the merry-go-round,
And pick at the lock, as the hands spin round,
Now the rhythm clicks to a quickening sound.
Tick tock too!
Tick tock, tick tock, tick tock, resound,
As the hands on the clock non-stop turnaround,

With gathering speed and clattering sound,
Tick tock, tick tock, tick tock, spellbound.
Tick tock to stop!
Ticka tocka, ticka tocka, ticka tocka, tock,
And tock follows tick, As tick follows tock,
To the never stopping, ever knocking ticking of the clock,
Going on tick-tocking, and tock-ticking to a stop.
Stop!"

Everybody remained silent after Peter's reading, grateful that he had not contributed yet another ostentatious and proselytising monologue, except John, who said, "Yes, very good. I also have been doing a lot of thinking about my life and my contribution is called, Faith and Fear; a piece of prose."

"Far along the narrow winding road filled with uncertainty, you may ask,
If there is a god; and is God's house closed to sinners?
The truth is that the world drags us all along the road to Hell.
The question is, can we channel our good intentions towards getting off this road?

If we are successful in diverting ourselves,
will we just find ourselves on a road to nowhere?
or will a new road lead to some kind of fulfillment or salvation?
Perhaps when you've trodden hard along all the other roads,
and can't see that any of them will take you where you want to go,
then the answer will become clear.
Move towards the light, reach out for it,
have faith, listen hard for a still small voice,
bid a firm farewell to the road to Hell, and choose eternity.
We come into this world alone and as nothing,
with nothing,

and for reasons only enlightened,
by faith in a god or faith in nothing at all,
while we are here, we search, hoping to find something.
And as we turn over stones in our search,
we don't always like what we find.
Perhaps the key is to turn over the right stones?
It is certain that one day you will turn over your last stone,
and then it's time to meet your spirit in the sky, to be gone.
We leave as we came, alone, with nothing,
except perhaps a faith in a God, or faith in nothing.
If there's a light at the end of the tunnel,
there may also be a tunnel at the end of the light."

"My God, that's heavy stuff," said Peter, "Where did you dig that up from, John?"

"I've been under a lot of pressure, not least of all because of being accused of murder. I sought refuge in prayer and trying to remain close to God and this came out in a rapid stream, one night just before bedtime. It took me only five minutes to write."

"Whatever rocks your boat." said David.

"I'm truly sorry for the aggravation and uncertainty you have suffered recently." added Stuart.

"Oh, please," snarled Peter, "God's an illusion, generated by people who are scared of dying. No more social services nonsense please."

A committed Christian was unperturbed by Peter's rudeness, while David and Stuart both gave John a sympathetic smile.

"And now," the great pretender uttered, in as derisory a tone as he could muster, "We await the eloquence of our friend writing a crime novel. You've had enough new material recently. What have you managed to write for us, Stuart, or were you too busy interrogating suspects to bother?"

After spending a few weeks with D.I. Pearson, being intimidated on a daily basis, the detective felt no need to respond aggressively to this snarled introduction. He just thought to himself, *"The last few weeks with Fearsome Pearson has got me used to being with bullies like Peter. He hasn't changed much despite the contemplative writings."*

"I've written a short poem, The title is "Time for a change". Here goes.

"Time for a change

Grandfather clock chimes out of tune
in a dusty corner of a musty room,
Old; out of time,
Bold, out of tune.
Nobody cares 'cause nobody's there.

Station clock hangs high and precise,
clicks chop the air and grip like a vice,
Loud, the moment hangs,
Proud it harangues
the platform crowd; insistent
clear and persistent,
Go home, go away, come back tomorrow,
or another day.

Alarm clock clangs a surly warning;
Once again, again it's early morning.
Rise and shine, raise your head,
go to earn your daily bread.
Jump aboard the money go round
Selling your brain on the gravy train.

Oh, let me be once again on a small red boat,
with large white sail, free and afloat,

no clocks, no time; just the sea and the sky, and me,
alone on the breeze, in a calm summer haze,
not counting the hours, or counting the days;
at peace, untamed, by the cursed chains of time."

"Oh, I like that. It describes the need for a beautiful, peaceful day in the turmoil of our daily lives." David praised.

"That's exactly how I have been feeling," agreed John, "I wish I was clever enough to write something like that."

The group leader considered that he should knock the praise down swiftly, but only because he was jealous of what Stuart had written.

"Not poet laureate standard, but pretty good, I suppose." was Peter's half scathing comment, "You need to try and make it more like Wordsworth."

Stuart's immediate thoughts were, *"I wondered lonely as a prat that sits so high on judgement hills.",* but he did not respond.

Throughout the meeting Davina had been silent and unsociable, locked in some sort of strange parallel universe, conversing with her Facebook friends. The other members of the writing group were used to her behaviour and now it was her turn to read, they feared another episode of the Blowjob Chronicles. They were to be perhaps disappointed and certainly surprised.

"Davina, it's your reading next." instructed the master of ceremonies.

She put down her mobile and without saying a word, began to read.

"If you were (flower, baby, lover)

If you were a flower,
Delicate and fine,
I would caress you with my hands,
Soft as morning dew,
Warm as summer rain,

Caress you with my hands,
Would you be my flower?,
You could hold my heart.

If you were a baby,
Naked and new-born,
I would hold you tender child,
Fold you in my arms,
Rock you till you slept,
Hold you tender child,
Would you be my baby?,
You could hold my heart.

If you were my lover,
Swore that you'd be true,
I would never let you go,
Hold you strong and near,
Give you all I have,
Never let you go,
Would you be my lover?
You could hold my heart."

Then, a few seconds later, she read a second piece.

"November Again

A day to remember, A time best to forget,
a love so dismembered, torn to shreds by regret,
a good time to pray, to say "I love you" and yet,
so many times to remember,
and never, never, never, never forget.
So many words passed between us today,
but all I ever, really wanted to say was "I love you".

For friends, who were lovers, we both lost in the end,
for Heavens above us, there's no need to pretend.
A love, so, so precious, but, a hurt that won't mend,
and so we, who were lovers,
are now only, now only, now only, now only friends."

Stunned, was the word best used to describe the reaction. For at least half a minute, no-one said anything. Then, with the exception of Peter, they all broke out into much relieved smiles.

"What no blow job!" thought David and then he said, "Davina, you've been hiding your light under a bushel. You can write excellent poetry and I think you should shy away from your Barbara Cartland romances, and concentrate on poetry from now on."

There was no reaction from Davina.

"Two poems and not a blowjob in sight, wonderful!" thought John. He added, "Written with such tenderness, I like it."

Still no reaction.

Stuart didn't know what to say. He was gobsmacked, so he offered, "I agree with that." while thinking, *"What's happened in her life for her to alter track so dramatically?"*

Frank did not offer anything. He had no time for romance. If he had developed the courage, he would probably have stuck his fingers in his mouth and feigned being sick.

Peter felt he had to react negatively, "It's not Christina Georgina Rossetti, but I suppose the pieces have some romantic value."

Davina's eyes bulged in their sockets and her fists clenched. Then she turned to Peter and spat, "You pompous twat! Nothing is ever good enough for you, but all you write is esoteric useless shit."

Before Peter responded, Frank came up with his favourite adage again, "Come on my friends, play nice. This is supposed to be a social group. We should be encouraging good writing, not criticising it."

Without a single reflection of remorse, Peter uttered, "Let's move on. What have you got for us then, Frank?"

True to form, Frank offered another very well written war poem.

"Kosovo

Homes blaze in the village, abandoned, destroyed,
Meagre possessions bundled crudely for flight,
Away scurried in haste to hide in the forests,
Past shallow quick graves of victims new murdered.

Tear-stained frightened children, with smoke-blackened faces
stare blankly eyes pleading in hunger and fear;
At once still relieved to be spared from the slaughter,
But fearful the future uncertain does stand.

No longer the peace of plain rustic existence,
The clock of the seasons, the harvest and plough,
Pale refugee faces tell tortured dark stories
as vanquished and beaten, they make for safe haven.

To the victors the treasure, fine wines in good measure,
Where death and destruction have won hollow gains,
To drive the sad peasants from the lands of their birth,
Their too willing war, genocide, and scorched earth.

With brutal abandon and killing at random,
So cruel and depraved the ground forces waged.
As tools of black terror raged death in green valleys,
Blowing wild through the land like the wrath of false gods."

"I remember that altogether too well," revealed John, "Terrible nightly bulletins on the news, all about genocide. You've captured the feeling wonderfully well, Frank."

"I'm a little too young to have more than vague recollections of what was happening," volunteered David, "But as a war poem, it is very moving and up to your usual standard. Man's inhumanity to man illustrated accurately."

"I like the juxtaposition of, "The peace of plain rustic existence, the clock of the seasons, the harvest and plough." against, "Tools of black terror raged death in green valleys, blowing wild through the land like the wrath of false gods.", offered Stuart, "It says all there is to know about the futility of war."

Peter's assessment had not been tempered by Davina's rebuke and so he couldn't help but be his usual self, "Hmm! another war poem," followed grudgingly by, "Quite good, I suppose."

There was no point in anybody telling Peter off again for his judgemental attitude. They all knew it was water off a very thick-skinned duck's back.

Besides which, it was a mere few seconds before Peter issued his next barb at David.

"What contribution can we enjoy or endure from our resident Sanderford millionaire?"

David explained that he had written a poem inspired by a midnight stroll along a Cornish beach. "Imagine," he asked, "Being five years old. It has been a lovely warm day. A glorious sun is about to sink into the sea and you suddenly find you're alone on the beach as the sky darkens."

"Lost Child

In the pale yellow light of a long seaside evening
On a nearly empty beach as a fading sunset dies,
Among the salty tasting tang of dampening sea breezes,
There calls an eerie, lonely sound that pulls my urgent gaze.

Under the lazy swoop and swirl of searching seagull glides,
Blurring at the darkened edge of softly lapping waves,

Along a sandy twilight waterline I faintly spy,
A lost child, solitary, crying by the sea.

Tears are smothered in the swell; cries are muted by the sounds,
She stands up and looks around, there's no one to be seen,
No one to be seen, no one to be seen.

Where are you my child? My Child where are you?
Where are you my child? My Child where are you?

And as the ever-moving hand of dark relentless night,
Sweeps away the last few rays of summer's dying light,
A growing mass of deepening shadows swallows up the sound,
And carries her away to be in the warmth of welcome arms.

Tears are smothered in the swell; cries are muted by the sounds,
She was lost, but now she's found, on her way back home,
On her way back home, on her way back home.

Bright day is soon abandoned to cool night's persuading charms,
Her failing soft hold now releases, crying ceases, she is safe,
And all remains in stillness are the gently lapping waves,
In worship to the restless spirits of creation and always."

It was getting late, and it had been a long and very concentrated session of readings. Comments were short but full of praise."

"Wonderful poetry, great words, felt like I was the child on the beach." said Stuart.

"It makes you scared and you want to know that the anguish is resolved in a good way." offered John.

"A fine piece of work." agreed Frank

Soon, they all packed up and went home.

Stuart sat in his favourite armchair with a glass of vodka and tonic and recollected how his companions had behaved that evening. In his private thoughts, he was looking for clues in the way the last few weeks had changed people.

"Glad that David was back with us. He hasn't changed at all as the result of the lottery win. He's a very solid, consistent character. As for Peter, well, he was the same picky little annoyance that he always is, but his writing was indicative of him thinking about time."

A mouthful of his ambrosia and Stuart came back to his innermost thoughts.

"John's obviously been worried a lot recently, when he couldn't find his alibi for the murder and he credits the resolution of that turmoil to his god. That's not entirely unexpected. Then there's Frank. He came up with another very good war poem, but there was something different about him that I couldn't put my finger on. The biggest surprise was Davina; no Blowjob Chronicles, just lovely romantic poetry. Either it's a temporary aberration or she has undergone some sort of epiphany. I wonder if I can read anything at all into the way they all conducted themselves. I'll sleep on it."

The glass was emptied and the bed was filled.

Chapter 34
Friday 30th November, Afternoon
Dilemmas

Tania was at Sharon's flat in Coniston Close, agitated and near to tears. Sharon looked at her sister and asked, "You seem a bit down, Sis', is there something the matter?"

She was expecting to hear that Tania was churned up inside about what had happened at Bridges a few weeks ago, and she was right.

"I can't afford my mortgage. I'm going to have to sell the flat and move in with you."

"OK, Sis, whatever you say. All girls together. Can't be bad. We'll look after each other."

"That's good to know, because I found out a few days ago that I'm going to need a lot of looking after soon."

"What do you mean?"

Tania burst into tears.

"I've just found out that I'm pregnant."

"Really! Oh, Sis, That's a shock. How do you feel about it?"

"How do you think I feel? I've lost my job, my flat and now I'm up the spout."

"Whose baby is it? Can you get him to pay maintenance? Be good if it was David Dimmock's baby, he's got plenty of dosh now."

"No, it's not David; I've never made love with him."

"Who is it, then?"

"I can't tell you. It would cause too much trouble for me and the father."

Brenda remained silent, reading a geology magazine. There was no way she would ever relate to motherhood; it just wasn't in her genes.

In Sanderford police station, there was more bad news when Stuart told Pearson: "I've got the results of John Wilson and Tania Thompson's DNA blood tests, and can confirm that the blood underneath Burrow's fingernails doesn't match either of them."

"You've done it again, Macca. Gone off snooping without my permission. For fuck's sake how many times do I have to tell you, I'm the lead detective on this case, and you...."

"What, Sir?"

"Just do as you're fucking told." in a raised voice.

Stuart smiled, "There are two things you should know."

"I should know everything." was the shouted response, accompanied by a fist banging on the desk.

"Number one is that you seem to have forgotten that you told me to get these DNA blood tests done."

"Are you sure?"

"Yes! And number two is that I had a chat with Superintendent Collingwood last night and he asked me how the case was going."

"You grovelling little tosspot." More fist banging.

Unperturbed, Stuart continued, "The Super' asked me to pursue these tests."

"They're totally irrelevant. They prove nothing."

"They may help to eliminate suspects."

"They only prove that there's no DNA blood match. They do not prove that the three of them weren't at Bridges murdering Burrows."

"I think we've already proved that, at least where David is concerned."

Pearson stood up and leaned aggressively over his D.S., spitting fire.

"All along you have been obsessed with eliminating suspects. The only suspects who fit the frame are your best mates, David, Pots-of-

Money, Dimmock, John, Drunk-and-Holy, Wilson and Tania, Such-a-Nice-Girl, Thompson. Everything you do convinces me that you are involved somewhere. I'll catch you out, Macca. You're going down with all your mates."

The D.S. laughed as his D.I. flew out of the room, swearing, "I've got work to do. Don't do or say anything more. Stay here and read the newspaper."

Pearson pulled up outside the gates of Sandersford mansion, feeling very pleased with himself and looking forward to pocketing a large sum of cash. Once he had penetrated the gate security and entered the building, he was greeted with a roll of the eyes from Terry Lennox. Mr. Big was just saying goodbye to Tania Thompson, who had visited him concerning her pregnancy. She left in tears; almost hysterical. It did not bother Pearson in the slightest. He gave it no thought whatsoever, because the only thing on his mind was collecting his money.

"Hello Inspector, I've been looking forward to seeing you. Let's go and sit down somewhere. I tell you what; you haven't seen my cinema room, have you? We'll go and sit in there."

The millionaire led his guest out of the hallway, across the lounge and into a darkened side room complete with video equipment and a massive screen.

"Sit yourself down, I know what you've come for." said Lennox standing at the back of the room.

"Let's not waste any time." Where's my money." insisted Pearson.

"Give me a minute. There's a scotch over there if you want to pour yourself one.

"No, thanks, just handover the ten grand and I'll be gone."

Lennox went out of the room leaving the D.I. sitting in the gloom. He returned a few moments later with a large brown envelope in his hand.

"Is that it?"

"First things first, Ian, first things first."

Lennox knew his visitor's christian name was Alan. He wanted to annoy him, but Pearson was impatient rather than annoyed.

"Stop fucking me about. Where's my money?"

The brown envelope was ripped open, and a video was taken out."

"What are you playing at? I've no time for games."

"Sit down and watch."

The video was loaded in the machine and when the picture came up, there was Lennox sitting in the hallway with Pearson standing up.

The sound was turned up and Pearson heard a familiar conversation.

"Burrows had this piece of incriminating evidence on you and was about to blackmail you if you didn't reinstate him."

"Really? That's very clever of you to fabricate that as evidence.

"I think the facts speak for themselves, and then there's the other document relating to the Neon Queens."

"What about the Neon Queens?"

"I suspect something shady is going on there too, but I haven't found out what yet. There is no doubt that sooner or later I'll nail you for that as well."

"Let me put a proposal to you. Can you turn a blind eye to the business with the demolition contract, if I come up with some useful information for you?"

"What kind of information?"

"Something that might help you with your investigations."

"The blind eye might come with a proviso. Do you understand? You paid ten grand to Frank Archer. I think it's only fair that you reward me with the same privilege. Shall we say that the two sums cancel each other out?"

"You'll have to give me a few days."

"I want it in cash."

"Is there any other way to give a bung to a bent copper?"

The video was stopped at that point. The look of horror on

Pearson's face was a delight for Lennox to behold, but there was persistence.

"Where's my money?"

"Shall I play you the video again? You don't seem to understand that what you said proves that you're a bent copper, and actually asked for......" Terry emphasised, "Asked for....."

"Asked for what?"

"Asked for payment for some information."

"You bribed me."

"No, I think you'll find that I did not offer you a bribe, only information."

"You bastard, I'll get your balls on a plate for this."

"I've got you by the short and curlies. Now you've seen the video, you can be sure there'll be no dosh for you. To use your own words, Detective Nobody Pearson, I've got YOU banged to rights now."

The disgruntled detective got up ready to leave.

"Oh, don't go just yet, Inspector. There's more to see."

Half-heartedly the detective sat back down.

"As you seem to have difficulty understanding things, I'll explain what comes next. I hope you enjoy this first bit of CCTV taken in the hallway. It shows Arnie and Lenny returning to the mansion on Thursday 8th November to play poker with me. Note the time stamp at 7.05 pm. Then there's another bit of video showing the three of us playing poker in my drawing room. Watch all of it if you like, but it will take a while. It's time stamped as starting at 7.15 and finishing at 10."

"But why did you bother to record all that?"

"It's simple. I hate losing at poker. So, I always record the games and watch them afterwards. First off to ensure nobody is cheating and then to watch very carefully all the mannerisms and facial appearances and to listen again to the way things are said. You've heard of the expression poker-faced, haven't you?"

"Yes, what of it?"

"It doesn't exist. If you study the way people behave when playing cards for money, there are always little giveaways, even how they breathe or what they do with their hands. If I record all the games then I will know whether a player has a good hand or not.

"That is cheating."

Lennox smiled, "I don't think so, it's science. I'm so sorry, but these bits of tape show conclusively where Arnie and Lennie were at the time of the murder. If you try to pin the death of Henry Burrows on my mates, these tapes will go straight to Superintendent Collingwood at Englesfield nick, got it?"

There was nothing more to say from the detective who had well and truly been caught with his pants down. He stumbled out of the mansion delirious with anger, got into his car and drove like a possessed demon back to his home, a converted barge, moored on the Cullington Quay. In the cold and uncomfortable galley of the Lady Pamela, he opened a bottle of Captain Morgan Rum and took two large swigs directly from the bottle. Over the next hour, like a runaway train heading for a derailment and in an unstoppable maudlin, rumbling temper, he proceeded to empty the bottle and drink himself into a drunken stupor. Then he tripped over on his way to the bathroom and fell asleep where he lay.

"It's all going wrong, wrong, wrong. I am the top man. Nobody gets the better of me, better of me. Bloody Terry, Terry Lennox, I'll get even with him, slippery bastard, jellied eels is right, slippery bastard. Thinks he owns Sandersford, Sanderford, Sandersford, Arsehole City. Closing Bridges, Burrows murdered, Bridges, Burrows, Dimmock. Dimmock can't be innocent, he's guilty, guilty, guilty, lottery win, money, money, money, guilty.

Wilson, holier than thou, God botherer, got angel's wings, ah, but still in the frame, ain't gonna fly away from me, no alibi ha ha ha, Tania nothing to do with it? Don't you believe it. She's no Mother Teresa. Arnie and Lennie, Laurel and Hardy, Another fine mess you gotten me into. Oh, No, no, no, no, no.

How did I get myself into this mess? It's a mess, big mess.

No! No! No!

Nobody outguns me, gunslinger that's me. McPherson, Macca, Macca, crap detective, outgunned, outgunned, outgunned. Macca, thorn in my side, elephant in the room. fly in my beer, turd in my Saturday, pain in the arse, arse, arse. He crawls up Collingwood's arse. Shut up! Shut up!

Softly, softly catchee monkey, softly, softly catchee monkey, softly, softly catchee monkey, softly, softly catchee monkey, wrong, wrong, wrong, wrong, wrong. It's all going wrong, wrong, wrong."

Chapter 35
Sunday 2nd December, Lunchtime
God Bless America

There were two vaguely familiar strangely dressed Americans, in the Feathers when Stuart, David and John met there for a lunchtime sandwich.

David looked over and after a moment's thought he recognised them. He didn't have to wait too long before the man in a red St Louis Cardinals baseball cap came over to him.

"Hi there, we met earlier on this year, on what you call Armistice Day. Remember?"

"Oh, yes, you must be Chuck and Darlene, on a whirlwind tour around Europe."

"You got it! We sure are having an interesting time, but sometimes it's a bit worrying. Let me get you and these good people a beer, and perhaps you can throw some light on my confusion."

"OK, we'll have three pints of Old Rustic Nectar Premium."

John interrupted, "No, make that a half a bitter shandy for me. I'm supposed to be on the wagon."

Chuck pulled a face, "What does on the wagon mean."

David clarified, "It means that he's avoiding drinking alcohol."

"I see, but isn't your bitter an alcoholic beer?"

"Well, yes, but a shandy means it's watered down with lemonade."

"Water, lemonade, beer, you folks do some strange things here in Olde Englande. Maybe we'll try that as well."

Chuck went to the bar and returned with a tray carrying the drinks.

He took one sip of his shandy and almost spat it out, saying, "My, oh my, that sure tastes like a heap of shit."

Darlene disagreed, "I think it's just fine and dandy."

David quaffed a large gulp of his beer and asked, "How was Australia then?"

"We were disappointed. It wasn't anything like the travelogue. We didn't see any koala bears or kangaroos and Darlene was disgusted."

"They all spoke German." she interjected.

Chuck continued, "There was a place they call the Spanish Riding School which wasn't anything like we expected. It was the worst rodeo I've ever seen. There were no bucking broncos, just big white horses prancing around like ballet dancers."

David kept a dead pan face, but Stuart was almost wetting himself with laughter as John nudged him as if to say, "What are these dumb Yanks on about?"

The American lady was working her way diligently through the shandy and paused to say, "One evening, we went to a Strauss concert, but Strauss failed to turn up."

There was no helping these poor ignorant Americans with their misunderstandings, so David changed the direction of the conversation.

"Anyway, what is your interest in coming back to Sanderford?"

Captain America replied, "My great grandfather, Joseph Snellgrove, lived here before he emigrated to the U.S in 1915. He was processed through Ellis Island and stayed in New York for a while. He was a carpenter and after a while, he settled in the Mid-west in St Louis, which is where we live today. We're going to meet someone called Andrew Snellgrove and he is a pastor at St Catherine's Church here in Sanderford. You guys probably know him."

"John piped up with, "Yes, I know him well, he's my minister."

"When we were last here, he wasn't around and that's why we have come back before we fly home."

"We don't have a pastor at St Catherine's," added John. "But you are quite right that the Reverend Snellgrove presides there. Why do you want to see him?"

"He's a distant relative and I hope he can show us some ancient records revealing something about Joseph."

Just at that moment, the Reverend arrived, took off his crash helmet, unbuttoned his leather jacket to reveal the dog collar and went immediately to talk to John.

"I'm sorry, John, I've been so busy that I never did get a chance to speak to you about the night I found you asleep in the park. It was bucketing down and you were drenched. I was concerned for you."

Flash! All of a sudden a small fragment of John's memory returned.

"Are you telling me that you saw me in the park that night after I got sozzled in here?"

"Yes, I woke you up and took you down to my church to dry off. You were in a really bad way."

"What time did you find me?"

"About 6."

"And what happened after that?"

"You passed out in the pews for the best part of two hours and just before eight you'd recovered enough to go home."

Stuart had listened to the interchange between the two men and was convinced that the Reverend Snellgrove was telling the truth.

Now he was relieved to find that John had a cast iron alibi for the time and date of Burrow's murder.

The Reverend looked over to where a St Louis Cardinals baseball cap stood out in the pub.

"Look, excuse me John; we can talk more at some other time. I've come here this lunchtime to have a chat with this American couple."

John went back to talking with David, "You look really pleased with yourself. Had some more good news?"

"Yes, I have. Not long ago I made contact with an old flame and went down to Cornwall for a few days to see her."

"Yes, you told me about what a lovely time you had."

"Well, Susan, that's her name, is just about to go to Philadelphia for a consultant's job and she's just called me on my mobile and asked me to fly over and join her for a few weeks. Only one small problem. I've got to find someone to look after Jeffery. Auntie Rose is alright for a few days and Jeffery likes it there, but I don't think she'll be up to looking after him for a couple of weeks."

Chapter 36
Monday 3rd December, Morning
Deepening Nightmare

It was an icy cold December morning. There had been a heavy frost overnight and some icicles were hanging from the rim of the slippery boat deck on Lady Pamela, the barge that was Pearson's home. It had been a weekend of tension, confusion and binge drinking, and waking up with a huge hangover in a small cramped bunk, hemmed in by damp walls didn't help. Still frustrated at not having been able to nail David, John and Tania, the detective had been on the edge of madness all weekend.

Reluctantly he crawled out of bed, shivering and cursing and attempted to revive himself with a lukewarm shower. He dressed, drank copious amounts of black coffee, nibbled at a few biscuits and smoked four cigarettes before leaving for work. His hangover was like the weight of a small planet balanced on a lolly stick. He ached all over, felt dizzy and sick and wanting nothing more than to shut out the world and crawl back to bed. With sore, bloodshot eyes and a streaming nose, he set off. He got into his Audi and drove into Sanderford sour-faced, dog tired and aggravated by the restless weekend he had endured.

He reached a set of road works on the Bellowmead Lane where the traffic lights were taking an age to change in his favour. Swearing and cursing at the delay did nothing to quell his impatience. The lights changed to green for a fourth time and this time he was determined to get going. Just to add more misery to his day and in an attempt to make progress, he shot a red light and crashed into the rear end of a dustbin lorry. His Audi was wrecked as the heavy lorry made mincemeat out of the front end.

The unfortunate result was that he suffered a suspected concussion. The dustcart lorry's driver called the police and an ambulance. It took them about ten minutes to arrive. Pearson was breathalysed and then taken to the Sanderford Hospital to be checked out. When he returned to the Police Station in the mid-afternoon, he was in an absolutely foul mood and unable to maintain any coherence with his reasoning. Not for the first time, a brooding silence pervaded the atmosphere in the room. In the circumstances, the D.S. decided it was an opportune time for him to take charge.

"Let's stop wasting our time chasing a hunch and look at the facts and the evidence so far."

"What stupid suggestions have you got?"

"Let us look at who we can eliminate from questioning and who may still be able to throw more light on the case."

"If we must."

"First, we'll consider who we can determine are no longer suspects."

"Fair enough."

"Both David and John have alibis."

"How's that? Dimmock's alibi from Brenda is busted. He says he was at home all evening."

"I'm convinced he was at home all evening and that the fifty grand he gave to Brenda was not for an alibi, but for her sex change operation."

Frustration showed on Pearson's face, but despite him still having doubts, he had to admit that the evidence clearing David from blame was pretty conclusive.

"John Wilson hasn't got an alibi. He must still be a suspect."

"No, I think we can also eliminate him now."

"Why?"

"I was in the Feathers on Sunday and was party to a discussion between him and the vicar, Reverend Snellgrove. Apparently, he found John asleep in the park at six and took him to St Catherine's to sober up. He says that John left to go home about eight."

"So Wilson has an alibi provided by the vicar."

"That's right."

After a nanosecond of boiling tension, the D.I. exploded with anger, thumping the table with his head, screaming at the top of his voice and sweating profusely. The D.S. was concerned that he might bring on a heart attack.

"Please calm down, Sir."

"Calm! I'll give you calm. You fucking sneaky, underhand wanker. You've destroyed the case. We don't have any leads now."

Stuart popped out of the room to get Pearson a glass of water and when he returned he pleaded quietly but firmly, "Listen, Sir, there is still work to do. We can solve this case together; co-operation is the key."

Pearson stood up and pointed a twitchy finger, "I've told you from the beginning, I do the detective work, you do as you're told and I solve the case."

"Please listen to what I have to say. You can take all the credit in the end. I've spent fifteen years as a detective and I'm used to not winning any medals. I'm still only a Sergeant for precisely that reason, but I'm not completely without ability."

"You want to get all the glory."

"No, Sir, I just want to help get this done and over."

"So do I. I'm growing tired of your interference and you're always sloping off to snitch to Collingwood."

"Let's get it over with then."

"You'll go on all day if I don't let you have your tuppence worth. Spit it out then, and make it quick."

"This is my assessment at the moment," Stuart said, "Tania is not a likely suspect and couldn't have carried out the assaults on her own."

"Yep, OK. Only together with others. Agreed!"

"Terry Lennox has got an alibi."

"I want you to forget about Lennox, anyway, and that's an order."

Stuart wonders, *"Why is he so adamant about that?"*

"Can we agree that Peter Thornton was not involved and knows nothing useful?"

"Yes!"

"So, where does that leave us and what factors do we need to re-examine?"

"You tell me, clever clogs."

"To make any further progress, Sir, I'm asking you to abandon all ideas about David and John. In short, I want you to capitulate with your original theory."

"Why's that?"

"I'm sorry, Sir, but you can't pin the murder on David, John and Tania, and I don't think we should pursue that line of questioning any further."

The D.I. turns quietly morose, as if he's been firmly and unfairly admonished. When he reacts he replies, "OK, if it's not them three, it's got to be another little gang."

"We can agree on that."

"So the question in my mind is, did Arnie and Lennie commit assault or murder."

"That needs to be looked at again."

Stuart notices a change of expression, as if a small realisation has just hit him, when Pearson retracts and says, "Let's not bother with that. I'm not really sure that they were involved at all."

Stuart wonders yet again, *"Why is he so adamant about that?"*

"I think we should interview Frank Archer concerning what appears to be an instance of him taking a bribe from Terry Lennox."

"That's something that could be difficult to prove. Leave it!"

Noticing an uncomfortable shiftiness in Pearson's demeanor, Stuart thinks again, *"He wants to brush under the carpet everything that connects with Lennox and his associates."*

"Move on, I'm getting fed up already."

"Yes, Sir. If we press Tania a bit, we should be able to clear up the mystery of where she and Brenda actually were at the time of the murder. This business about Brenda allegedly being in two places at once is still worrying me. I'm convinced that she was not with David and he did not assault her and inflict that gouge on her cheek. The evidence and testimonies we have so far can confirm that."

"She says she was at Coniston Close with Brenda and Sharon."

"That may be true, but it may not be the whole truth."

"Then there's Sharon. She may be lying or bending the truth about where she and Brenda were."

"Yes, that absolute bitch, Brenda. The only way to get any sense out of her will be to arrest her for obstructing us in the execution of our duty. She was aggressively uncooperative when we saw her down at Chilverton. She may also be hiding something."

"It would be interesting to see the result of a DNA blood test on Brenda. The scratch on her cheek might undermine what she declares were her whereabouts, if it turns out to be a match for the blood under Burrow's fingernails."

"If it matches she's in the frame."

"Yes, and did you know that as a geology fan, she has a rock hammer."

"When I talked to her she suggested I arrest all geologists for the murder."

"It seems unlikely that the fatal blow was struck with a rock hammer, but the injuries to Burrow's hand and knee could have been inflicted with it."

Chapter 37
Tuesday 4th December, Late Afternoon
Tightening the Ring

It was the afternoon of another long day, resplendent with two warring detectives. Pearson lit a cigarette, took a long haul and made a decision. "Right, Macca, I think that now it's time for us to talk to Tania, Sharon and Brenda."

"Probably better to catch them all together. I know that Brenda will be working at the Poundshop. I don't know about Sharon. She's unemployed and on benefits. As for Tania, I heard on the grapevine that she's recently moved in with Sharon. They may both be at Coniston Close."

"What time do you think Brenda gets home from the Poundshop?"

"Probably about 6."

"Right, we'll go over at about 5.45 and talk to Tania and Sharon first. That bitch Brenda will only cause trouble from the start if they are all together. If she turns up while we are already there, it'll probably set her on edge and that may or may not be beneficial."

Tania answered the door at Coniston Close. She looked as if she had been crying. Pearson ignored her sorry state and said, "We need to talk to you again. Can we come in?"

Stuart asked, "Is there anything wrong? It will just be a few questions for clarification."

Stuart was welcome, but Pearson wasn't, nevertheless Tania said, "Come in, if you must."

The detectives sat down on the couch across the room from

Tania's armchair, Sharon sat at the dining table. Stuart began with, Tell me, Tania, where do you live now?"

"My flat is in Sunderland Drive, but after losing my job, I've had to move in with my sister Sharon here in Coniston Close."

Pearson interrupted impatiently, "Where were you on the evening of 8th November?"

"I left work at shortly after five. Mr. Burrows had just sacked me. First of all, I was at home, then I came over to Sharon's. We were having a girl's night in."

Sharon added, "Prosecco and Pizza."

"What time did you arrive at Coniston Close?"

"Don't know exactly, maybe about six."

Sharon again, "That's right, Sis. We were in all evening, weren't we?"

Stuart noticed that Sharon seemed to have a need to confirm everything that her sister said, but Tania didn't answer.

"Were both Sharon and Brenda here with you?"

"Sharon was at home, but Brenda wasn't. She arrived later." said Tania.

Sharon added, "Brenda came straight from David's place. They'd had another row. She was here about 6.15."

Stuart enquired, "OK Tania, can you tell me if she had a scratch on her cheek?"

The answer came with the slightest hint of hesitation, "Yes, I, er, think so."

Pearson snapped in, "Did she have a scratch on her cheek or not?"

"He scratched her cheek." insisted Sharon.

"Are you telling me that David scratched her cheek?"

After another flash of uncomfortable hesitation, Sharon said "That's what she said."

This was a most peculiar version of good cop, bad cop and there were only vague answers to the questions raised. The junior detective jumped in and began talking to Sharon.

"After Brenda arrived, what did you do?"

Sharon raised her voice, while Tania shuffled nervously on her chair, "Like I said, we were all drinking prosecco and eating pizza."

"Where did you get the pizza from? Did you make it or order a takeaway?"

"It was a takeaway from Domino. I'm a regular customer there."

"Delivered or collected?"

"We collected it?"

"About what time?"

"About 8 or 8.30 ish."

Pearson was a bit short, "Why did you go out to collect it when you could have had it delivered?"

"I wanted to see my friend, Cheryl, who works there."

"But you had been drinking. Did you drive there?"

"Don't be stupid. I'm on benefits. How would I afford a car?"

"So did you all walk or did one of you drive?"

"I don't remember. Perhaps Brenda drove us there. I don't remember. We were all a bit pissed by then."

"So what you're saying is that Brenda drove to Dominos after she'd had a bit too much prosecco?"

"I don't know. You'll have to ask her."

The D.I.'s eyes glazed over and rolled. He was becoming frustrated with the lack of certainty illustrated in the answers. He looked at his D.S. who retook control.

"Previously, you said that the three of you had been in all evening. You didn't mention going out to collect a pizza. Why?"

"It must have slipped my mind."

"So, let's recap. Between 6.15 and 8.30ish all three of you were together here, except when you went out to Domino's to collect pizzas."

"That's what I said."

"A few days after 8th November when I met you outside Davidsons Newsagents in the High Street, you said that the three of you were at home all evening."

"Yes. Do you have to keep repeating what I said?"

"But Brenda says that at that time she was in Newcastle Gardens being assaulted by David. And later she claimed that David had inflicted the wound on her cheek. There's something confusing about the timings here. Can you help?"

"What do you mean?"

"Brenda was in two places at the same time."

Just at that very moment, Brenda arrived.

"What in the name of fuck is going on here?" she hurled, "Why are you two useless fuckers bothering us again. Get out!"

Stuart did not rise to the challenge. He calmly stated, "We have some questions to ask you and it is most important that you co-operate or we will need to take you all to the Station."

"For fuck's sake, haven't we done this all before?"

"Just clarifying some points." replied Stuart.

"OK, but be quick, it's beginning to stink in here and you're not going to pay for the fumigation, are you?"

"I must ask you to clarify something.." Pearson stated, looking straight at Brenda. "Where were you at 7 pm on 8th November?"

"I was at home being assaulted by David."

"And who inflicted the injury to your cheek?"

"David!"

"That's not what your friend Sharon says. She says you were here."

"So what? Maybe one of us has memory problems."

"So, you don't remember where you were?"

"Maybe."

"So were you here or at David's?"

"Don't remember."

"You were quite clear a moment ago."

An angry reply followed, "Can you remember precisely everything that happened a month ago?"

The realisation that the investigation was going nowhere began to annoy him and Pearson was spitting fire. He got up and began kicking the wall and shouting at all three girls, "What is it with you bitches? Why can't you just tell the truth?"

Sharon was silent and expressionless. Brenda smiled a wicked malevolent smile. Tania's eyes filled with tears, her shoulders shuddered and then she stood up, ran around the room, with her hands over her ears and started to scream.

Stuart wanted to console her, but it wasn't strictly in the rulebook. He approached her and she frantically waved him away. Pearson was unmoved. He seemed to be enjoying the distress he had helped to bring about.

"I'm making some coffee." said Sharon calmly, leaving the room and remaining in control of her senses, while Brenda paced up and down looking like an angry dragon spoiling for a fight.

"Why don't you both fuck off and leave us alone? We've answered all your questions," she shouted, "Get out! Now! Or I'll chuck you out myself."

There was a minute's deepening silence. Neither detective moved, although Stuart was feeling distinctly uncomfortable.

"You'll have to excuse me," uttered Pearson in exasperation, "I have to go out to my car to make an important confidential phone call."

"Good! Don't come back." screamed Brenda, "And take your pathetic little sidekick with you."

After a few minutes, Pearson returned and declared, "I want you two to have DNA blood tests." pointing at Sharon and Brenda.

"Why?" Brenda replied.

"It's routine after an assault. It may help us to eliminate you from our enquiries."

"Why not Tania as well?"

"She's already had one."

"Really!" and turning to Tania, "Why didn't you tell us that?"

"I'm sorry," said Tania quietly, still sobbing, "But I didn't think it was important."

"I refuse!" snarled Brenda.

"So do I!" repeated Sharon.

"Are you girls hiding something?" Stuart asked politely.

"What have we got to hide?" sneered Brenda.

"Then you'll have the DNA blood tests. As required, tomorrow."

"How's that?" Brenda asked.

"When I went out to the car, I contacted our nick and requested that we get some DNA blood tests done on the two of you tomorrow morning at 10 am."

"You can't do that."

"Yes, I can. Look! You have a choice. Come to the police station for DNA blood tests tomorrow morning or we'll come and arrest you. That's the gist of it."

Sharon and Brenda looked intently at each other and then Brenda shouted, "Why don't you fuck off and die. You bastards! I'm leaving."

"You can try, but I've got two officers outside this house who will arrest you the moment you attempt to go."

That wasn't true, but Pearson smiled. Now he was certain he had the upper hand. He was beginning to enjoy confrontations with Brenda and was now convinced that he was close to learning the truth at last.

"Do you understand?" he said.

"Yes! Now get the fuck out of here, before I kick your balls and chuck you out." spat Brenda.

Stuart got up promptly to go, while Pearson enjoyed deliberately moving slowly towards the door.

"We'll have the results by tomorrow afternoon. Stay at home and wait for us to contact you. We may need to take you in for further questioning."

"Oh, fuck off!" said Brenda.

Chapter 38
Tuesday 4th December, Late Evening
Review

It was late evening and the two detectives were back in the interview room at Sanderford police station. The D.I. lit a cigarette and leaned back in the least uncomfortable chair.

"We've got them, Macca. At last we are going to prove that at least, some of those three bitches are involved in the murder. My money's on Tania and Brenda, probably with Dimmock's help."

"That's your hunch, is it? I think that is very unlikely, Sir."

"The proof of the pudding, Macca, the proof of the pudding."

"Let's just look at motive, means and opportunity for a minute." said Stuart.

"Oh, that old fashioned bollocks again," declared Pearson derisorily, "Then it'll be softly, softly catchee monkey. You don't give up with your antiquated ways of solving crimes, do you?"

"Let's just do it. Please, Sir."

"OK, if we must."

"Let's begin with Tania."

"Tania: motive: yes, being sacked. Means: probably, capable with assistance. Opportunity: likely, again with assistance. Don't tell me again what a nice girl she is. She ain't the Virgin Mary."

"Alright, Brenda."

"Brenda: motive: no, none apparent, but she is a nasty piece of work. Means: yes, remember the rock hammer? Opportunity: likely, given her vagueness about timings."

"I said before that I don't think the rock hammer was the murder weapon."

"Who's the senior detective here? Move on."

Sharon, then."

"Sharon: motive: yes, Burrows was her uncle. She was sexually abused by him when she was a child. Means: perhaps, with Brenda. Opportunity, likely, given her vagueness about timings."

"I think that was a very useful exercise of clarification." asserted Stuart.

"It was bollocks! Have we finished? I've had enough for the day."

"How about personal assessments of these three, then?"

"Oh, for fuck's sake, get it over with."

"When we went to Coniston Close recently, Tania was in a right state. She cried, went hysterical and I suspect she was being forced to cover up something. Brenda was, and is, relentlessly antagonistic and I wouldn't put it past her to act violently in any circumstances. Sharon is a bit of an enigma. She is probably mentally scarred from the sexual abuse she suffered. The relationship between her and Brenda is clearly one where Brenda is dominant. Perhaps she is easily led?"

"If you have quite finished, I'm going home. See you tomorrow for the blood tests."

Stuart had some other ideas up his sleeve, so before Pearson got up and left, he said, "Excuse me, Sir, but I'd like to have the morning off tomorrow, I've some very important things to do."

"What are you up to, Macca, snitching to Collingwood again?"

"No, Sir, let's just call it family business. I've been neglecting my usual duties, and I feel I must catch up."

"Oh, well, I suppose so, once these DNA blood test results come through, we'll be finished, one way or the other."

"What do you mean by that?"

"Either we'll have a positive match or we'll be back where you keep pushing us again."

"Where would that be?"

"Ship wrecked with no suspects or back with me, thinking that you murdered Henry Burrows. Anyway, I'll solve this case without your help and despite having to tolerate your hindrance. I don't care whether you are there or not."

Stuart refused to respond and quietly left the interview room.

Stuart returned just after lunch the next day and found Pearson in the interview room. Smug and self-satisfied were insufficient to describe his demeanor. By the thickness of the smog and the intoxicating nature of the stench, it appeared that the D.I. had been indulging in several celebratory cigarettes,

"Nice of you to grace me with your presence, Macca. Had a good morning, licking Collingwood's arse, did you?"

"No, Sir, I've been extremely busy with a piece of detective work of my own."

"Trying to find out why all the ducks have disappeared from Willow Tree Park or was it more important stuff like who kicked over a waste paper bin by the River Sander?"

"Neither, Sir."

"That probably means you didn't solve the mysteries, because you are a shit detective, who couldn't find a pound coin in a bag of pennies."

"If you say so, Sir. Perhaps we could now attend to the matter of Henry Burrows murder."

"Yes, let's. Without your help I have solved the crime."

"Have you, Sir?"

"The DNA blood test results are back and there was a positive match between the blood under Burrows' fingernails and the sample given by Brenda."

"I see, Sir. That places Brenda at the murder scene on the evening of 8th November and confirms that Burrows scratched her face. The scratch would indicate that there was some sort of altercation between the two of them."

"All right, Miss Marple, that's enough stating the bleedin' obvious. Let's go and get that bitch and all her mates, first thing tomorrow morning. I'm going to enjoy seeing her crumble. Then we'll go and pick up Dimmock before he buggers off to Cornwall again."

Chapter 39
Wednesday 5th December, Afternoon
Disappearance

It was just after 2 when the detectives arrived at Coniston Close, Tania was there alone. They sat down on the grubby couch while Tania sat herself on a kitchen chair.

"Where are Sharon and Brenda now?" Stuart enquired.

"They've gone. I heard them planning it when they were loading the car yesterday."

"Planning what?"

"Sharon and Brenda left the country yesterday afternoon. I overheard them saying they were travelling to France and going into hiding."

"Do you know why they've absconded?"

"Er, no!" hesitantly and looking away furtively.

"I think you do, Tania. It's time for you to tell the truth, please", Stuart asked gently.

Pearson had already decided he was going to arrest Tania and now he butted in, raising his voice aggressively, "Tell the truth now or we'll arrest you for suspected murder and for refusing to reveal your accomplices."

Tania began to sob uncontrollably. Stuart took a box of tissues off the table and put them on Tania's lap. Pearson remained impassive, almost oblivious to the distress Tania was experiencing. The young girl's mind was in a turmoil. She had lost her job, had been forced to abandon her flat and recently found out she was pregnant. The father didn't want to know. She began to imagine life in prison with her baby and the sobbing continued for a while, until she decided what was the best thing to do.

"Give me a few minutes to compose myself and gather my thoughts and I'll do what you ask." she declared quietly.

Tania got up and went to the bathroom. The two detectives sat in silence staring into space; very different space. Stuart felt extremely sorry for Tania's predicament, whilst Pearson relished the idea of putting her on the spot and wheedling some kind of confession out of her.

After a full ten minutes, during which the D.S. remained calm and confident and the D.I. fidgeted and fretted impatiently, Tania returned. Her eyes were red, her makeup was smudged and her face was pale. She cleared her throat and began, "The whole scenario of what happened on 8th November has haunted me for weeks. It has become so over stamped on my memory and been repeated in my thoughts so many times, that I am able to remember very well, precisely what happened."

"You'll accompany us to the police station for questioning, then." insisted Pearson.

"Do I have any choice in the matter?"

"No, none at all. Either you come with us willingly or we will arrest you. Get your coat on and stop wasting any more time."

Back at Sanderford Police Station, the discussion began; three people crowded into a small, stuffy, smelly room, two sympathetic with each other and one with vengeance on his mind. Pearson lit a cigarette. Stuart bought in a pot of tea and two cups, for himself and Tania.

"Ok, let's talk about the evening of 8th November. You've said that you were at Sharon's all evening drinking prosecco and eating pizza. Is that true?" Pearson began abruptly.

"Not entirely. We were there early on, but we started talking about me being sacked by Mr. Burrows and it got out of hand."

"What do you mean by that?"

"Brenda was already wound up after her argument with David and when I told her about me being sacked at Bridges, she was furious. It's no secret how hot headed and irrational she can be sometimes. Sharon is always so easily led by Brenda and decided it would be fun to go to the office and smash things up. I was reluctant, but because I had the keys to let them into the office, she and Brenda became very persuasive. They'd both already had quite a bit to drink. I didn't want to go, but at about 7.20, we drove over there. We sat outside for a while and then before we went in Brenda took her rock hammer out of the boot."

The D.I. was quick to cling on, "So Brenda murdered him with several vicious blows with the rock hammer." It was a statement, not a question.

"No, that's not what happened."

Stuart looked sternly at Pearson. He decided to intervene, "I think it's best if we just let Tania tell us what happened in her own words and in her own time, without supposing or suggesting anything."

Just for once, Pearson didn't protest, he just sighed, "Oh, all right. But let's get on with it."

"Please continue. Take your time."

"We went into the office at about 7.30. Brenda and Sharon had been swigging from a bottle of prosecco in the car and getting more and more steamed up. We didn't expect there would be anyone there, but strangely the office wasn't locked. When we went in, it looked like Mr. Burrows had already been attacked. He was crawling up from the floor. His face was bruised and bloody. He was groggy as if he'd been asleep or maybe unconscious for a while. I thought that perhaps he had overdosed on Paracetamol, because they were spread all over the desk and floor."

"What happened then?"

"When he saw the three of us, he became nasty and abusive."

"Do you remember what he said?"

"I remember only too well."

"He said "What's this then? Is it the three witches from Macbeth? Double double toil and trouble, fire burn and cauldron bubble, eye of newt and toe of frog.", then he laughed.""

"And then?"

"First, he rounded on Sharon saying, "I can see who has got the eye of newt.""

"She was spitting fire, replying, "You filthy paedophile pervert. You forced me to give you a blowjob when I was just 8 years old, you abused me at every opportunity, and raped me when I was 11. I fucking hate you. You bastard.""

"He smiled a wicked evil smile and said, "What you remember is pure fantasy. I never touched you, you stupid ignorant bitch. Look at you. No one will come near you with a barge pole.", and then he went on, "As for pervert, well, look at you with your tattoos and piercings and confusion as to which way you swing. Even when you were a little girl, you were such an ugly little fucker."."

Pearson interrupted, "So that's when she hit him with what, the paper weight?"

Stuart gave Pearson a stern look again, hunched his shoulders and pleaded, "Please, Sir, let Tania tell us what happened."

The D.I. didn't react. The D.S. asked, "Can you continue, please."

"Next, Mr. Burrows rounded on Brenda, saying, "You're obviously the toe of frog, but that's an insult to frog's toes, because they are clearly more intelligent than you. You're just a no-hoper, an aggressive, selfish bitch; nasty, vindictive and lacking any sense of decency."

Brenda went ballistic and started waving the rock hammer about, banging it on the table and shouting and swearing. She was out of control. "

"Did she hit him with the rock hammer?"

"No, not at that stage."

"What then?"

"He started on me, saying, "As for you, Tania, you're the bubbling cauldron, who shags anyone with a pulse. I doubt if there is a man in Sanderford you haven't tried to screw. You shagged every bloke who ever worked here. You're nothing but a sex crazed, whoring man eater. What's more, I know about you and Terry Lennox. You are all three slags, bitches and perverts."

"What did you do then?"

"I started to cry."

Tania stopped explaining and took a deep breath; tears filled her eyes and her hands were shaking. When she had recomposed herself she said, "The whole business was getting a bit out of hand. I wanted to go home. I didn't want to hear any more insults. I remember saying, "I'm going home. Now." Then Sharon said, "Don't be stupid, Sis. We are all in this together and we can't let him get away with this." That was when things got much worse."

"Did you do anything?"

"No, I was absolutely terrified of what might happen."

"So what did happen then?"

"Sharon was so riled up that she found a golf club on the floor and swung it round in the air, shouting, "I'll kill you, you bastard!", and then she hit him underneath his jaw. He yelled, "Oh, you fuckin' bitch.", and she yelled back, "You sick perverted child molester.""

"So, now we've at last got to the important stuff," said Pearson with a self-satisfied grin.

Tania ignored him, and went on, "You know all about Sharon and Brenda's relationship. So it wouldn't surprise you to know that at that point, Brenda needed no persuasion to join in. She started to smash up the room with the rock hammer. Burrows tried to stop her and they grappled, and Mr. Burrows struck out at her, scratching a deep gouge in her face. He is obviously no weakling, but he was suffering quite badly from the previous beating. Brenda went absolutely mental and came at him with the rock hammer banging it on his right hand, saying, "This is for what you did to Sharon when she was a little girl.", and then she hit him again with the rock hammer on his left knee."

Stuart listened carefully to every word; what was said and how it was said. While Pearson, beamed with delight. Here he was with the case sewn up at last. He was ready to go in for the glory.

"Can you go on?" asked Stuart.

"Yes, Mr. Burrows must have been dizzy. He started swaying as if he was about to fall to the floor. He was howling like a dog and that was when it happened."

"What?"

"Sharon was urging me to have a go. She said, "Go on, Sis, give the bastard a whack for all the times he's treated you rotten.", but I was in tears and refused to join in. I was horrified at what Sharon and Brenda had done."

A deep breath, "Sharon picked up the golf trophy paperweight and delivered a blow to the right side of his head and after that, he fell down. By that time, I had crawled into the corner of the room, crying. I just could not believe what was happening. I'd been persuaded to join in with the stupid idea of smashing up the office and here they were attacking Mr. Burrows."

"Do you think Burrows was dead then? Had the blow with the paperweight killed him?"

"Perhaps! We didn't hang around to find out. Anyway, I'm convinced that Sharon and Brenda would have just kept hitting him until he was dead."

"Was that it?"

"No, before we left Brenda told Sharon to wipe the paperweight clean. Then she picked up the golf club again and said she was going to throw it in the river. Then we left."

"What time was that and where did you go?"

"It was about 8.15. We went to Domino's and got some pizzas and then went back to Sharon's. They both carried on drinking. I was too shocked to eat or drink anything."

"Thank you telling us what actually happened, Tania. Would you be prepared to testify in court all you have just told us?"

"Yes, I think so."

"Is there anything else you want to say?"

"Well, I remember a discussion about making sure each of us had an alibi. Yes, Sharon told us to invent alibis, just in case. She thought that the Paracetamol all over the desk and floor would help to confuse the issue and that maybe whoever beat up Mr. Burrows before we arrived would end up being found guilty of his murder. She expected for her and Brenda to get away with it. Brenda decided to report an assault on her by David as an alibi. Sharon couldn't work out an alibi at that time and neither could I."

"OK, now tell us what happened the next day. You found Burrows dead in the office is what you claimed first of all."

"I was so troubled and couldn't work out what to do. After a restless night full of demons, I decided to go to the office the next morning and claim that I was there to retrieve my umbrella, which I had mistakenly left there the previous evening, after Mr. Burrows had sacked me. That would give me a reason to be in the Bridges office and to look as if I'd discovered Mr. Burrows' murder."

"When you got to Bridges?"

"I tripped over the paperweight on the floor and without thinking put it back on the desk. When I thought about it later, I realised that the only prints on it would be mine. That would be suspicious because there should've been some prints from Mr. Burrows. By the time I'd realised how stupid I had been, it was too late. Anyway, there and then, I decided to phone the police and ambulance."

"If that is all, Tania, I'm sorry but I'm afraid we're going to have to detain you at the police station for the time being."

Chapter 40
Friday 7th December, Morning
Wrapped Up

Overnight, there had been some developments and investigations. It had been confirmed that there had been an ANPR sighting of Brenda's Ford Ka at Dover. The car had been on the 17.10 Stena Line ferry to Calais. Foolishly, Brenda had used her credit card to buy a one-way ticket for the crossing. Police had contacted the bank immediately and put a block on any future transactions. Sometime later the French Police had discovered Brenda's vehicle abandoned in a layby just outside Lille. The runaways had walked into town and found the railway terminus. There had been an altercation between the ticket office and Brenda when she had tried to buy two single tickets on the TGV to Lyon, and her credit card had been refused. Sharon had left her mobile in the car, thinking that she shouldn't use it any more in case the telecomms company could trace her whereabouts. Brenda had persuaded her that they should return to car, collect the mobile, and use it to purchase their fares. At the ticket office the desk clerk had reported the argument with Brenda to the local Police. When Brenda and Sharon returned to the railway station, the French Police arrested both of them. Arrangements were swiftly made to have them shipped back to Sanderford. At 10 am the next day, they were escorted back, handcuffed, tired and disheveled, into a cell in the Police Station.

Pearson and Stuart were sitting in the small room discussing the murder case that they now knew they were close to resolving, when they were advised that Sharon and Brenda had been returned under escort from France. During the journey back to England, they had confessed to being at the Bridges office on the night in question.

"I wonder why I have always been a little bit suspicious of the three girls' involvement in this case?" asked the D.I.

The D.S. thought to himself, *"Yes, of course you have. That is why you followed your hunch about David, John and Tania so ardently. You were wrong and if you were honest with yourself, you'd admit it. How convenient for you that you have now changed your mind. Great detective work, I must say."*

What the D.S. said, though, was, "Yes. From the way that Brenda and Sharon behaved when we talked to them and the reluctance to submit themselves for a DNA blood test, I'd say that they must have been involved somehow. But I still can't believe that Tania has taken any part in a murder."

"Because she's such a nice girl?" derisorily.

The dig was ignored.

"The results of those DNA blood tests do suggest that Brenda was at the murder scene and that perhaps, during the attack on Burrows, she sustained the gouge on her cheek."

"I'm certain that Brenda was at the murder scene and that's where she got that bloody gouge out of her cheek. It's her blood under Burrow's fingernails, we've got the bitch cornered and it's only a shame that we can't put Dimmock back in the frame as her accomplice and the murderer."

"He has an alibi. Whatever way you look at it, perhaps he has two alibis; but which one is true? We've been through this before. Remember me saying, was he at home watching the football, or was he at home assaulting Brenda, or was he at Bridges? My answers to those three questions still are, yes, he was watching football, no, he didn't assault Brenda, and no, he was not at Bridges." The look on Pearson's face was one of resignation to Stuart's assessment.

He sighed, "Whatever! I told you I would crack it in the end, didn't I."

"Yes, Sir, indeed you did, but you spent a long time following your hunch and barking up the wrong tree trying to put David, John and Tania under suspicion."

"That's what real detective work is all about, following hunches, even if in the end, they don't bear fruit. It doesn't matter anyway; I got there in the end. You just delayed the outcome with your wishy-washy ways of investigating."

Stuart smiled. He had good reason to avoid a totally unnecessary argument about the Henry Burrows murder case. Fortunately, at that point, the phone rang and the D.I. picked it up. The conversation was over quickly.

"That was Collingwood. He wants to see us right away. Let's go."

They climbed into a taxi and headed for the Englesfield police station. Pearson couldn't resist having a smug dig at his D.S.

"You see? Collingwood is very pleased with me and wants to give me a slap on the back. You're just coming along for the ride."

"Of course, Sir, that must be why he called us."

The Englesfield division H Q occupied a modern 3 storey block in the centre of the market town. The two detectives took the lift up one floor to Superintendent Collingwood's office. Lots of light through the big windows and a smell of disinfectant contrasted greatly with the dingy atmosphere of the interview room at Sanderford nick. The boss was immaculately coiffured and shaven, dressed in a smart grey suit, blue police shirt and black tie, with expensive and very shiny black shoes, all of which added to his air of superiority. Pearson disliked that intensely.

The Super' bade his two officers to sit and said, "I knew this would be a very difficult case and that's why I put the two of you together, because I was sure that eventually your two different approaches to detective work would pay dividends."

"It was a difficult case, Sir, but I managed to overcome all the difficulties. Another one to add to my excellent clear up stats." smirked the D.I.

"It needed both of you to work together to reach a satisfactory conclusion."

"And I got there in the end."

Stuart sat there smiling, silent and placid. By now, he was well used to Pearson's attitude. The Super' smiled back and sat back comfortable in his chair and with his hands clasped behind his head.

"I think congratulations on a job well done are in order for clearing up the case."

"Thank you, Sir." replied the D.I. with a satisfied grin, "They don't call me Fearsome Pearson for nothing."

"Detective Inspector, I have to tell you that I was very annoyed with your attempts to have D.S. McPherson removed from the case."

There was no reaction.

Collingwood continued, "However, I know that I was absolutely right to keep the two of you together."

Pearson wobbled and shuffled in his seat wanting to disagree. After a few seconds, he said, "Local knowledge may have been useful, but...

He was abruptly cut off by his superior officer.

"Local knowledge and an understanding of the characters of the people in Sanderford were vital to solving the case."

The response was tiresome Pearson at his most arrogant, "But the real detective work was in sniffing out the culprits and putting them behind bars."

"Agreed that we must always succeed in putting people who commit crimes behind bars. It's a shame that we were unable to achieve that easily in this case, but given the time and a little assistance from Interpol, we succeeded eventually in developing a prosecution. "

"Thank you for your recognition of my ability to do that, Sir."

There was no response.

"Anyway, it was a well-earned success. I know it was a difficult investigation."

Both, "Thank you, Sir."

Anticipating that they have finished talking, the detectives got up to leave.

"Just one more thing before you go. Would you both sit back down for a moment, please?"

They both sat back down, while the Super' leaned forward in his chair to provide an emphasis.

"Stuart's been doing a bit of extra digging, and has found out some interesting things."

"Really? He's been working behind my back again." Pearson thought while he was seething underneath.

"Yes! And he's going to get a commendation for it."

"And what do I get, then?" asked Pearson, his attitude boiling up inside.

"Oh, nothing much to worry about. Two things actually,"

"Two commendations, then?" he joked.

"I'm afraid not. I've seen your recent breathalyser results and they confirm you were drunk in charge of a motor vehicle at 9.30 am on Monday 3rd December. That is not quite the behaviour I expect from officers in my division."

"I can explain."

Collingwood held up his hand and grinned, "There is no need, Alan. I understand."

"We can cover that up then. Can we?"

"No, I don't think so."

Pearson scowled.

Collingwood was about to relish the next moment, "You see, Alan, old chum, there's more."

"What do you mean, Sir?"

"It saddens me to tell you that you could be going down for taking a bribe."

"No! But, but, but...."

"We've been keeping an eye on you for a while now. Nobody likes a bent copper. I'm afraid that you may have lost your job, sacrificed your pension and brought shame on the services we endeavour to provide to the public."

"No, you are kidding. Tell me this is a wind up."

"I'm afraid it's not. We've got solid evidence of your crime, provided by a very reputable source; someone who lives and works in Sanderford. You do know Terry Lennox, don't you?"

"Yes, of course." A pause. *"Reputable?"*

"Well. The moment you leave this room we will need you to help us with our inquiries."

For once a very black-faced D. I. Pearson was speechless. Inside he raged about being caught out, and worse still, by his companion on his last case, none other than the shit detective, Stuart McPherson.

Collingwood added, "I could leave this to the boys from the fraud squad, but nowadays I don't get much chance to say it."

"Say what, Sir?"

"It delights me too much to have the opportunity to say. "Alan Pearson, you have been arrested under suspicion of taking a bribe. You do not have to say anything, but it may harm your defence if you do not mention when questioned something you later rely on in court. Anything you do say may be given in evidence." Do you understand?"

At that moment, the relentless bully that was Alan Pearson had nothing to say. While Collingwood grinned from ear to ear, the D.I. was hang dog."

"I'll take your silence as a yes, then."

Superintendent Collingwood sat back in his chair with a rueful smile, "Ex Detective Inspector Pearson, I wish you good luck in your future exploits. Did you know that the people who hate a bent copper most, are his fellow inmates in prison?"

Later that day Tania had been released and received a call from David.

She told him everything that had happened and then started crying again. "I've had to give up my flat because I can't pay the mortgage.

As you know, I moved in with Sharon and Brenda, but now they've done a bunk to France, I'm going to be homeless again. Sharon's place is owned by the Sanderford Housing Association and it won't be long before they find out she's gone, and chuck me out on the streets. I really don't know what to do."

There was a brief pause while some wheels turned in Newcastle Gardens.

"You may be able to do me a favour then."

"How's that."

"Well, I'm going to the U.S.A. for a few weeks soon and I need someone to look after Jeffery. I've got a spare bedroom and you can move in as soon as you like."

"Are you sure that won't be a problem, David?"

"No, don't be silly. You'll be helping me out by looking after Jeffery and just think of it as me returning the favour."

"And when you come back?"

"Perhaps you will have sorted out somewhere to stay by then, but don't worry, you can stay at mine as long as you like."

"Oh, David, you are so kind. Thank you so much."

Chapter 41
Friday 7th December, Late Afternoon
Loose Ends

Superintendent Collingwood lounged comfortably in his upholstered chair. He had examined a whole wad of important papers on his desk.

"It was a real can of worms, Stuart. A sleepy little back water like Sanderford and eight possible arrests. Bringing criminals to justice in the service of the law-abiding public: that is what police work is all about. Well done!"

"Thank you, Sir."

"However, I wonder if we could spend a few minutes examining each case and determining if we have sufficient evidence for prosecution."

"Yes, Sir, I am keen to discuss that with you."

"OK, here goes! We'll look at the murder of Henry Burrows in a few minutes. If that's OK with you?"

"As you say, Sir."

"Well, first of all then, Terry Lennox. We've got him down for bribing a council official, but with all his money, he'll probably hire the best lawyers and get off on a technicality. We'll be keeping an eye on him though and if he steps out of line, we'll have him."

"Trouble is he's much too smart and he's got other people to do the dirty work for him and take the can."

"Yes, I agree."

"In his favour, I suppose, is that he did enable you to collar D.I. Pearson."

"We'll have to see what the jury comes up with when it goes to court."

The Super' switched to the next document.

"Next, it's Frank Archer, and his transgression is taking a bribe. But we know that there are some council officials who might be tempted to stray from the straight and narrow, especially if they've got financial problems."

"Well he's been with the Council as a planning officer for about 15 years. He used to work at Bridges, so there was a connection between him Henry Burrows and Terry Lennox. I know a bit about him from our writer's group meetings, but the idea of him taking a bribe was a big surprise to me."

"That's as maybe, but if we can't get Lennox for offering a bribe, it would seem to be unlikely that we can get Archer for taking one. Again, we'll have to see what the jury comes up with when it goes to court."

"So, he might get away with it as well, if Lennox can wriggle out of it."

"We'll be watching him too."

Collingwood was summarizing the situation perfectly and Stuart was confident that his extracurricular investigations without Pearson's knowledge were considered important, even if there was some doubt about achieving convictions.

"Now, better possibilities or should I say probabilities?"

"Who do you want to look at next, then?"

"Arnie Spencer. He has admitted aggravated assault."

"Easy one. I expect he'll go to court, plead guilty and take his punishment."

"Likewise for Lenny Blunden, who has admitted GBH. He already has a criminal record and seems to be the sort of character who thoroughly enjoys beating people up."

"Well, he has done it all before, hasn't he?"

"As you say, we can expect he'll go to court, plead guilty and take his punishment. He'll probably enjoy a little spell at Her Majesty's pleasure."

Stuart thought to himself, *"So far, two possibles and two definites."*

"Now we look at the Henry Burrows murder, and we have three possibles for involvement. First of all we have Tania Thompson. What's your thinking on her?"

"She had the keys to the Bridges office and has admitted to being there with Brenda Taylor and Sharon Thompson. From what she has told us, I think she was not involved in the assault or the eventual murder. She was perhaps an unfortunate victim of circumstances, easily led by the other two, but not really a participant in the crime itself. When we get the other two to court, she will be a useful witness."

"Yes, and by all accounts I think we can rely on her for turning Queen's evidence. I understand that she has given you a full account of what actually happened at Bridges on 8th November and precisely who did what, with what, and when."

"Yes, Sir, she's made a full statement."

"So to the gist of the matter; the murder itself. Does Tania Thompson tell us exactly what Brenda Taylor did on that night?"

"Yes, Sir. We should be able to charge her with GBH at the very least, maybe attempted murder and possibly with murder."

"What about Sharon Thompson then?"

"Again, GBH at the very least, maybe attempted murder and possibly with murder."

"These two together committed the crimes. Interpol have handed them over, so now we can bring them to justice, preferably sooner rather than later."

"Perhaps we had a bit of good fortune there, but by the time the French Police picked them up we already knew that they were involved in the murder of Henry Burrows."

"Well, it looks like you've made a clean sweep in Sanderford, Detective Sergeant. Your commendation will be forthcoming."

"Thank you, Sir, but aren't we forgetting someone?"

"If you mean D.I. Alan Pearson, we certainly won't be forgetting about him. I'm interested to know what raised your suspicions about him?"

"Well. Every time I tried to get near to Terry Lennox, or Arnie Spencer, or Lenny Blunden, he pushed me away, saying leave it, that's an order. He kept using his favourite phrase, to warn me off talking to them."

"And what's his favourite phrase?"

Stuart replied with a grin, imitating Pearson's attitude perfectly, "Who's the real detective here? I do the detective work and you do as you are told. Understand?"

Collingwood laughed, "Fearsome Pearson, an arrogant bully boy who always wants all the credit for solving crimes. Got him banged to rights now."

"I was suspicious of his motives, and did some digging on my own and unknown to him." Stuart smiled but pretended to be sorry, "I'm afraid in doing so I didn't follow his orders, Sir."

"Never mind. Good work! Well done!"

Other Titles by Michael Haley
Published in Great Britain by Mirador Publishing

Chelmsford 2012 - Many Hearts - One Mind
ISBN 978-1-910104-76-7 (Novel)

First City of Essex - Many Diversions One Destination
ISBN 978-1-910530-04-7 (Novel)

An Idea Appeared
 ISBN 978-1-910330-64-1 (Poetry)

Turning Over Stones
ISBN: 978-1-911044-46-8
(Poems, Song Lyrics, Stories and Recording History)

Angel's Rainbow
ISBN 978-1-912192-44-1 (Novel)

A Little Collection of Short Stories
ISBN: 978-1-913264-17-8 (Stories and Poems)

Tall Words on a Wall
ISBN: 978-1-913833-10-7
(Poems, Song Lyrics, Stories and Recording History)

The Old Dog and Duck Chronicles (Novel)
ISBN:978-1-914965-10-4

Coming Shortly
Walls came Tumbling Down
(Poems, Song Lyrics, Stories and Recording History)

Printed in Great Britain
by Amazon

82908049R00120